SHADOWS & DECEIT

Betrayed, Uncertain, Relentless

A Novel

By

Kevin M. Scott

ISBN:
978-1-967632-48-0 **E-book**
978-1-967632-46-6 **Paperback**
978-1-967632-47-3 **Hardcover**

Those who knew then still know, and I thank you.
Those who didn't believe still exist, and I thank you, too.

TABLE OF CONTENTS

PART 1

MISSION: LAS VEGAS

The intel on the CEO's departure was flawless. Cire was already in position, minutes away from splattering the CEO's blood and brains across the hotel sidewalk. I was positioned on the adjacent rooftop, serving as Cire's spotter and assigned to clip the CEO's sole security guard. I checked in with Cire to ensure he was on point.

"Four mils from the target is a small patch of Honeysuckle. Confirm?" I asked, eyes steady through the scope.

Cire took a beat to respond. "What color are the honeysuckle?"

"Orange."

"Confirmed," Cire responded. "I see orange honeysuckle."

"Copy."

Las Vegas was the perfect place for this mission—clear skies, scorching heat, and not a hint of wind to throw off a shot. At this hour, the Strip was quiet. Most revelers were still dead to the world after a night of excess, or shuffling toward breakfast buffets, their sunglasses hiding their shame.

At exactly 6:42 a.m., a royal blue Bentley Flying Spur slid up to the hotel entrance. Two minutes later, the CEO stepped through the sliding glass doors, his svelte bodyguard at his side.

"Thirty," Cire murmured in my earpiece, his countdown always precise. He never spoke again after the thirty-second mark unless it was critical.

"Copy."

That's when my phone buzzed.

TARGET: BG, not CEO.

I had seconds before the radio silence. "New target bodyguard, not CEO. Confirm?"

"Say again?"

"The bodyguard is our target, not the CEO. Repeat: Bodyguard, not the CEO."

There was a pause, then Cire's voice came back, clipped. "Confirmed."

The chauffeur was the tell, stepping out in a textbook black suit and tie. He crossed to the guard—decked out in a blue-and-white Fendi tracksuit and spotless white sneakers—flashing money instead of subtlety. They shook hands, exchanged pleasantries, and lined themselves up like marks on a range.

Cire's timing shifted with surgical calm. He was free to take the shot.

"Send it!" I called.

The shot was fired, and a single bullet pierced the bodyguard's center mass, blowing him back into the double doors. Glass shattered behind the man, and chaos ensued in the guest arrivals section of the hotel.

"Splash," Cire said, indicating his work was done.

The chauffeur dropped to his knees, shouting over the dying man. The CEO's face twisted in terror as he bolted for the Bentley. Both men dove inside, the car fishtailing hard as it tore past the parking structure in search of cover.

Panic rippled across the scene. Valets scattered like roaches under a kitchen light, while others sprinted into the street. A handful of onlookers crept forward instead, phones raised, eager for footage.

"Target down."

"And he ain't gettin' up, Bruv," Cire responded in his dry, UK tone.

CONCERNED

Lies. Truth. Pride. Deceit.

I never thought what I did was terrible, but sometimes horrid things happened. When the jobs came, I moved discreetly, providing whatever support was needed. Long removed from an umpteen-year military career, jobs were still identified as 'missions' or 'operations.'

One thing never changed: I never jeopardized my family.

Whatever the case, I had one confidant. Salvatore. We discussed war and peace, love, sports, and business simultaneously, all in the same breath, always in the same place, out of habit.

Trust was the question. Did I trust Sal too much? Did I reveal too much—or anything at all? Maybe I didn't even trust myself. Psychologists were out of the question. There was too much hype about "mental health." Some shrinks tell you to listen to your heart or trust your gut. I trusted Sal. Maybe too much, but I could tell him anything. He was my go-to psych. Most leaders don't have a trusted number two guy who isn't gunning for the number one spot, but Sal was my number two from day one.

I beat the rush-hour traffic and arrived early at our favorite wing spot, Buckets. The lull between lunch and happy hour made the place feel calm, like the sea just after a wave breaks. The sports bar felt peaceful like after a wave crashed on the beach.

The bar was separate from the general seating area. In the public seating area, you are at the mercy of the servers' table count, especially if the server is having a bad day.

I wondered why most people didn't congregate at the bar more often, but figured it was innate for individuals to sit at a table, just as they would at home.

An older gentleman sat to my left, two stools over. He wore an off-blue suit, a crisp white dress shirt, and no tie, or he had taken it off to unwind. He swirled amber scotch in his glass, phone in hand. When I walked up, he motioned for me to sit. His slight turn away suggested he wanted privacy. Fine by me. People feared my presence less if I broke the ice—but this one clearly wanted none.

The bartender was attractive, and once Sal arrived, I knew he would drool over her, proposing a trip to a place where they served frozen drinks and little umbrellas or anything else to keep her attention. He'd leave a generous tip so she'd remember him.

Sal's attention-seeking maneuvers demonstrated his love for the opposite sex like an addiction. I doubt it would ever change, even if he settled down. Not that he would cheat on his wife or anything, but for Sal, it was the thrill of the hunt—the chase. Like or be liked. Kill or be killed. Can't have it. Don't want it.

She introduced herself as Gina, but her name tag said "Janice." I squinted, raising one eyebrow, but didn't say anything other than that I was waiting for a friend. I asked for water with lemon, lime, and no ice. She called me 'fancy.'

Above the shelves of vodkas, cognacs, whiskeys, and liqueurs, there was an assortment of sports-related games, shows, and news. I concentrated on replaying the Rockets-Timberwolves game and texted Sal to let him know I was seated at our usual spot.

The suited man swirled his scotch, eyes locked on American Ninja Warrior—United States versus the world. I smirked at the irony. Wasn't America supposed to be the melting pot?

The show made no sense to me, as it was about which country had the far superior gymnastic obstacle course. I focused on hoops and waited for my buddy.

Sal sauntered in, waving at people he didn't know, and flopped down on the barstool to my right. He wore an olive Adidas tracksuit and white Stan Smith tennis shoes, smelling as if he had bathed in orange peels. It wasn't overbearing but evident. He dapped me up, finished with a fist bump like we always did when we saw each other, and asked which TV I was watching.

"Replay of the Rockets game," I said, pointing to the TV slightly to my right and before him.

"I like the French guy on the Timberwolves," Sal stated. "He's a workhorse. Doesn't take any shit, ya know? He just comes in, blocks shots, dunks the ball, and plays his position because he knows his place. A good player knows his capabilities and limitations and combines them with his skills, ya know?"

I did a double-take. "Are we talking about basketball?"

"Life and sports often parallel each other. I'll explain when you're older, my son."

"Gee, I appreciate it, Dad," I said, pointing towards the bartender, "and I think you're going to like this one." Gina/Janice walked up and greeted Sal.

"Hi, handsome," she said. "You've had your friend sitting by himself for a while, waiting for you. I hope you had a good excuse."

Sal attempted to maintain a straight face, staring at Gina/Janice. She was his type. I knew how Sal liked them: medium height, slim build to a degree, petite but thick in the right places like a volleyball player or a sprinter.

"Oooh, la la! Look at you!" Sal teased.

The server blushed, and Sal continued, "I don't have to give my best friend any excuses," he said. "But, I do have a reason, if you must know. I watched this new cop series on Netflix and got caught up—good guys versus the bad guys. I cheer for the bad guys, but Netflix doesn't allow you time to digest what you just saw before the next episode comes in six or seven seconds. Maybe less, ya know?"

The waitress laughed. "Oh-em-gee! You know, I was just telling the same thing to my sister, Janice. It's crazy you say that."

"Ahhh haaa! Sal grinned. "You've got a twin?"

Gina's expression suggested she exposed a private, secretive code.

"Wait, how did you know I was a twin?"

I tapped my left pec muscle, and Gina looked at her name tag. She looked, smiled, and moved closer to Sal and me for the big reveal, flashing some cleavage. Sal took several snapshots with his eyes.

"Yeah, she and I both work here. The boss thinks it's hot. We are twins as well as bartenders. We get hit on a lot, so we'll switch name tags. If a guy comes in asking if we remember him, we're not lying if we say 'No.' It keeps things exciting and fun around here for us. We laugh about it at home."

"So," Gina changed the subject, "are you handsome guys just drinking water or something stronger?"

Sal and I ordered wings and fries. Sal asked Gina to surprise us with one of her specials. I asked for another refill of water with lemon and lime. She returned with a drink called 'Green Tea,' consisting of Jameson's whiskey, peach schnapps, triple sec, a splash of Sprite, and green liqueur.

I sipped mine while Sal gulped his.

"Damn, this is good shit, Gina. Bring me two more of those. What other tricks do you have up your sleeve besides being a twin?

"As a matter of fact, how come this is the first time I've seen your exquisite self? My guy and I come in here all the time. Are you mostly on days or weekends? Tell me something amazing about yourself."

"Dang, what's with the twenty questions?" Hands-on both hips, she winked at Sal and refilled a customer's glass with the soda gun.

"Going in for the kill so soon?" I asked.

"Nah, man. You know me; I'm just being friendly, but she is fine. Like that dancer who used to be married to the ball player."

I had no response.

Sal smacked the table in delight. "Teyana Taylor! That's who that cutie looks like with her fine self. Shorter, but still cute. Now that I know she has a twin, I'll tell Cire and see if he wants to double-date. I've never seen her or her twin. Have you? Hmm."

I shook my head as Sal was calculating our visits.

"Cire would consider this slumming; plus, you're probably twice her age."

"Never stopped me before. Or them. I'm harmless, you know?"

I elbowed Sal in his ribs. "Just promise me you'll name your firstborn after me, OK?"

Women were a complicated distraction for Salvatore, and he found it enjoyable. Our line of work didn't allow us to establish long-term bonds. I was the anomaly with a wife and a daughter, but I married young - before our business, missions, and operations.

We watched hoops in silence, sipped another round of green whiskeys, and waited for our wings to arrive. Sal was more talkative with food in front of him.

"So, everything OK at home?" Sal asked.

I twisted and puckered my lips. Before I answered, I set the mood by telling Sal I called my yard guy. I was upset with the gardener because he wasn't there and always came on the last Friday of the month.

"Today is Thursday."

"Yeah, I know that, brainiac. I woke up Tuesday thinking it was Wednesday, and my days have been running together for no apparent reason. Or there's a reason I haven't figured it out yet, but I felt like a total jerk for treating this guy like that. He's a nice man. Always smiling. He loves what he does."

Sal faced me with a wrinkled forehead.

"So, everything is or ain't isn't OK at home?"

"Ain't isn't?"

Sal sneered, "I said what I said. Ain't isn't."

I held my shrug to my ear for an extra beat and forced a smile. It was a smile of hysteria, like running through a red light. I didn't have an answer, and it was too soon to speculate.

I could tell Sal anything. Friends, since our senior year in high school, we learned that the Air Force Academy accepted us.

Strangely, I didn't recall seeing Sal in school before that meeting. Sal was my best man at my wedding.

I inhaled and held it for ten seconds, wanting my lungs to burn. Exhaling released the tension in my shoulders, and I revealed, "Something's up with Alana."

"Something?"

"I can't put my finger on it, Bro. It could be nothing, though—you know me. I'm usually right about my hunches. She's different, I don't know—distant even if she's standing in front of me."

Sal sipped. "What woman isn't different? They are delicate, precious, beautiful, psycho, temperamental, and frickin' different. I love different women at different times, but I'm crazy. The crazier they are, the wilder they are in bed. Want me to put a shadow on her?" Sal asked.

"What? No! Hell no, man. Shit, that's excessively next level, Bro. She's not one of our marks. She's my wife, man."

"OK, Oh to the K," Sal casually responded, like he didn't offend me. We watched the screens in our respective hush.

"I'm not sure, man," I broke the silence. "She could just be occupied with work, but lately, something has distracted her. She does not come home and chat about her job, tell me who's driving her up the wall, or how her bipolar VP can't decide about their projects.

"She doesn't complain about the skinny IT guy who smells like vodka or her burly director who wears tight shirts and smells like Axe cologne spray. She used to complain about being the only woman of color in the department and how her counterpart should retire, but sleeps at his desk. It's just home, shower, dinner, bed, wake up, work out, shower, and get dressed for work early and out the door.

"Maybe it explains why I called Ernest about the yard," I continued, rubbing my temple. "She usually mumbles something about the shrubs after a run, but I took the silence as an attitude. Know what I mean? She's in, and she's out. Sara's picked up on it, too."

Sal threw back another shot of his whiskey and slammed the glass down. "Fuck that, Bro, she's getting a shadow," Sal shouted, which got a few patrons' attention. He shifted closer to me. "I like Alana, but you're my brother, man, and you don't deserve that shit. Sara is either with her cute, innocent self. With this green concoction, you and I could be chillin' in a hot tub with Gina and her sister, Janet."

"It's Janice, and the drink is called Green Tea. What about Cire?"

"Janet, Janice, whatever, and C can care for himself," Sal huffed. "He's got plenty."

Sal took his cell phone out of his pocket, scrolled briefly, and thumbed a message. He took a sip, spun on his barstool, and observed another server until they made eye contact. She smiled. He waved. She waved back, and he winked with a nod of approval. She blushed.

He studied her more until some businessmen walked before him on their way out. He spun back, smiling, and drummed his fingers on the bar. His phone chirped. He looked down, punched in response, and put his phone back in his pocket.

"Splash."

"Hot date?"

"Nah. Radar."

Fear set in.

Sal maintained a relationship with his wild-card buddy, who had a bizarre history. Legendary stories about Radar were akin to sightings of the Loch Ness Monster, aliens in Area 51, or Bigfoot in the Redwood Forest.

I never met Radar, but I heard he was a crafty genius with his projects, gadgets, and weapons. Rumor had it that he was a no-nonsense assassin and ghost as resourceful as any Black Ops agent. Depending on who told the story, Radar was likened to James Bond and Jason Bourne, but with an evil spirit.

"I'm speechless and a little concerned, Bruh."

"Radar is semi-retired now," Sal informed me. "You have nothing to worry about. Plus, he likes you."

"Me?"

"Yeah, you, who else? He said you have a big brother vibe about you; he likes."

"We've never met."

Sal waved me off.

Anyway, he caught a bullet at a gig in New Zealand about a year ago. It spooked the shit out of him. Some paranoid billionaire forgot who he hired and had an extra security detail. Intel was all jacked up; the left hand didn't know what the right hand was doing, and pffft! Chaos. Ray was in a fucked-up position and felt compromised. First time catching a hot one, ya know?

"The Great Houdini got caught, so he's off the grid even more; almost stealth, but he responds to his crew, especially me. Cire's worked with him a few times, too."

"Wow." I thought about the target Cire took out in Vegas, but that man was deader than Elvis Presley.

"Yeah, man. But this type of shit entertains him, keeps him busy, and it's risk-free. He's number two on our next gig, so you'll meet him, but maybe you should sit this one out until you get your head right around Alana."

"No can do. Deposit already hit the account, and Cire is out on intelligence gathering."

"Who's the point?"

"C."

Sal contemplated. "Fuck it, but if your head ain't in it, bro, abort."

Showing no teeth, I turned to Sal.

"So, Radar knows me, and no one informed me?"

"Business decision," Sal said, drumming his fingers again. "Radar's circle is molecular. I just told you he's off the grid, a ghost. It's all good. Be glad he likes you because he's not a 'like-a-lotta people' guy."

Both chameleons, he and Radar, could blend in anywhere with anyone - like changing radio stations. Sal could vanish for weeks and show up at our wing spot right on schedule.

"So, your punk ass was late because you were watching something on Netflix, Bro?"

"Man, I swear those shows just keep going and going," Sal proclaimed. "I get it now when people say they've binged-watched seasons without moving. The shit is addicting, man."

I shook my head and laughed. The distinguished man to my left laughed, and Sal laughed at the man in blue.

STRESSED

Two weeks later, my wife was still in stealth mode. Our conversations were clipped, her presence distant. When I left for the mission with Cire, all I got was a quick peck on the lips. Nothing more.

It was the first time we'd been assigned a female target—reason enough for Cire to run point. Sal said I was a walking billboard for married men, and my disposition would blow any mission. I guess my swag wasn't like it used to be. Meanwhile, Cire was the guy who walked off the cover of Muscle Mag, GQ, or Esquire. I always envied men from the UK. It's like they were born wearing a Windsor knot around their necks and a high acumen for color schemes.

Our mark was Diatta, the alluring assistant—and niece—of a Senegalese ambassador who suspected her of treason. Senegal's close partnership with Saudi Arabia on the Yemeni border made this betrayal a matter of international urgency. The ambassador's team had intercepted encrypted messages proving her disloyalty. Diatta was supposedly on holiday in Los Angeles, but she was really rendezvousing with her accomplice. The ambassador wanted it handled.

Cire made contact with her through social media and a dating app. I played his chauffeur.

I landed at Hollywood Burbank and headed straight to Dr. Joshua Goyle. He handed me the kit. Goyle had a reputation from Guantanamo Bay—specializing in serums that made detainees suffer hallucinations: sudden drops in blood pressure, the terror of falling, visions of bears, lions, even deities. They always broke before they died.

I picked Cire up from LAX. He'd been rendezvousing with Diatta at the W in West Beverly Hills. Cire scoped the area in advance and nodded; it was perfect. It surrounded tourist attractions, including Rodeo Drive, where he'd taken her shopping. I was more interested in Ripley's Museum, and Cire gave me a hard time.

"You're such a kid." He laughed.

"I know it's corny, man, but it's my thing," I shot back.

"This should be easy as pie," Cire said. "After we shop for the umpteenth time and she thanks the hell out of me in bed, we've got dinner reservations at STK Steakhouse. I'll get her nice and full, and we'll get a nightcap at the bar before we return to the suite."

"Spare me with the other details, C. I know how you operate - especially with the ladies."

Cire smiled. "She's fine, Bruv. Have I shown you her picture yet?"

Cire opened his photo app to reveal the woman.

"Damn! What's her name?"

"Diatta, but that's not important. She's got to go. I'd put her on my team—maybe even starting five. I'll make it quick."

"No," I said, handing Cire Dr. Goyle's serum. "This will make it quick."

"Copy that. I prepped a suicide letter, so it appears she took herself out from the guilt of betraying her uncle and her country."

"I've manipulated the interior and exterior cameras around the hotel, so we'll be fine from that standpoint."

Cire gave me a thumbs up, "Never doubted you, player.'

"Oh, I'm the player?"

"You're the guy, Bruv. I like how you flow - like a true leader. We all trust you, Bruv," Cire retorted in his Brixton accent. "Especially when we got business."

I looked at the woman's picture again. "How can someone this fine be so deceptive to her own country, not to mention her uncle?"

Cire responded in the queue. "Money and blood don't mix, but the serum does the trick, and the serum is the fix."

"Are you reciting, Biggie?"

"And here I thought that was a Harry Belafonte original. Anyhow, Bruv, let's get this done so we can enjoy LA while we're here."

"I need to get back home for Sara's swim meet. I like being there as much as possible, especially with Alana flying in another stratosphere lately."

Cire nodded his head. "Respect. Tell her, Uncle C said good luck at the meet, and I hope shit works out with you and Alana, Bruv.'"

An hour later, I waited for the artificial couple to show up. I saw Al Pacino Walk out of the hotel with a woman who could have been a model or someone famous. Straining my neck like a typical stargazer, I studied the man with salt-and-pepper hair and a limp gait. Then, a wave of people by the door froze in admiration of Cire, and Diatta approached the SUV.

She was wearing the hell out of a lemon chiffon, deep-V, low-cut dress with a ruffled front and ruched back, and it teased anyone with eyes of her goodies, as if they were begging to escape the fabric. She represented Africa well.

C was pissed, but he, too, looked like he walked off the cover of a magazine wearing a classic black Sid Mashburn suit, a black Bellissimo fedora, and aviator sunglasses. Someone could have mistaken them for a celebrity couple and taken his picture with this woman with all her body parts exposed - right before she's about to meet her demise at night's end. Matching his anxiety, I swooshed the SUV out of the valet area. It reminded me of our escapade in Las Vegas.

As I had imagined, the hit went as planned, with dinner, drinks, and execution by means of a death serum. Cire texted me: SPLASH, and I knew it was done. I drove back to the airport to head home.

ANGST

The LA hit made me think about bugging Alana's phone. A software tech could commit adultery if a diplomat's niece betrayed her country and family, potentially provoking war. I wasn't sure if tapping the phone would interfere with Radar's investigation, and it solidified that I no longer trusted my wife. When I returned from LA, I thought things would have been better, but we'd grunt *good morning* before her run and huff a *goodbye* before leaving for work.

She and Sara increased their conversations, but the foundation of those chats was deliberations about what Sara was attempting to wear to school, swim practice, and meets, or going over to a friend's house on weekends.

Sara was our only child. Alana and I discussed having two or three children before we married. It didn't matter either way because, as a man, I was not enduring the physical aspect of carrying a child. Hell, menstrual cycles perplexed me. I held an unselfish stance and took nothing for granted as I learned pregnancy and delivering a baby were separate and different events for mothers. Sara's entrance to the world was frightening.

Alana was 38 weeks pregnant, considered full-term by her OB, and was doing great. She maintained a rigorous workout regimen to ensure she did everything right for herself, the baby, and her physical well-being. She ate all the right things and didn't have weird cravings unless a peanut butter and jelly sandwich every four hours counted.

When Sara was born, Alana texted me to meet her at the birthing center. I was both excited and uncertain because this was outside of our delivery plan.

Upon my arrival, Alana was in bed with straps and monitors attached. She indicated she could not catch her breath but felt the baby jolt inside her for two hours straight. She said she'd never experienced those kicks or sensations and sensed something was wrong. The delivery team conducted some tests and performed an ultrasound, capturing images of the baby. After seeing Sara wrapped around the umbilical cord, the doctors got her out quickly.

Alana and I both thought she had delivered a stillborn. Sara was unresponsive for the longest seven minutes of my life. I would have traded anything to relieve her of any affliction, but I chimed in with her when I heard her first cry.

Alana remained in the hospital for a week with Sara. Doctors introduced themselves as specialists for this body part and other medical professionals for my wife to ensure our baby was OK from her initial shock at the world.

As much of a blessing as babies can be, I refused for my wife and me to endure any stress again. We'd be happy with our one gift and alleviate additional suffering. It was the first time I felt helpless and useless.

TENSED

One morning, to kill any doubt that Alana was screwing around on me, I walked up behind her and hugged her. If she shrugged me off, that would be a sign. She was standing in our bathroom, wrapped in a towel and still wet from the shower. Facing the vanity mirror, her smile gave me a sense of security. We swayed back and forth, and I kissed her neck. She moaned in agreement, shuddered, and found my hands on her waist. I moved them up to her whole breast and pulled her closer to me, grinding on her so she could feel my hardness.

My right hand moved down her waist, swirling my fingers around her *special place,* as she called it. Her breathing was heavy, and she reached behind to grab onto me. She untied the drawstrings of my lounge pants, and I stepped out. We made our way to the bed and made love for the first time in over four months. It was good, no, great for both of us.

Our breathing was coordinated, like we had exchanged a baton during a 100-yard relay. We enjoyed each other's bodies for two other mornings in one week, and I felt better about us. She was chattier in the mornings but still maintained her same routine, giving me disingenuous pecks on my lips on her way to work.

I consulted a preacher friend for some marriage advice. I found his name and typed a text message. I erased the first message and plucked in a different note. It didn't read right either, so I deleted another one and three more messages before I determined to work it out.

I punched in Alana's work number, and she picked it up after the first ring.

"Well, this is a surprise. Is everything OK?"

Hearing her voice made things OK, but I wanted to know.

"Yes, everything's fine," I lied. "I just wanted to hear your voice. You've been scooting out pretty quickly in the mornings. Are you good?"

"Oh, I'm just busy with work stuff, and this project I'm working on is almost over," she said. "There are lots of moving pieces, but it's coming together. I'd tell you about it, but it's dull work stuff."

"Cool, cool. I know you've got it under control. You should be running the place. Listen, I'd like to return to being us again if this makes sense to you."

There was a beat of silence before Alana responded.

"Of course, Dear. Of course, but I must go. My next meeting is starting, so I will see you tonight, OK? Love you, bye."

Alana came home earlier than usual and pulled out the stops. She let Sara stay at a friend's house, which was a sign that it was going down on a school night. She prepared broiled salmon glazed with honey and garlic, which I liked. She included baked red potatoes, asparagus, and white wine. Alana surprised me with my favorite, which is *only on special occasions*, spiced rum pecan cheesecake. It was her Lola's Filipino recipe.

I was working my way from the narrow end of the slice to my third forkful when Alana got up from the table and whispered, "When you finish your slice, there's more dessert for you in the bedroom."

I finished the slice and devoured my wife.

The following day, Alana got up for a run.

Radar and I established an expedited bond after Sal contacted him. I remember sending him a text, informing him that if he found out Alana was involved with another man, he would let me know immediately. Otherwise, I didn't need to know anything about her movements at work, so I let it go. I wanted to be fresh and stress-free for our next gig. Radar agreed and never informed me of any ill behavior.

A week later, my phone rang.

The caller ID stated UNAVAILABLE. Most of the time, I didn't answer UNAVAILABLE calls, but the rule was to send a text first, then call, and I had already received a message from our liaison, Jevaun.

"Yo."

"Yep."

"You him?"

"I'm him."

I detected someone who disagreed with this in the background, but the man on the phone was the shot caller. His sense of command and order gave me the impression that he was seasoned.

"Can you come now?"

"Where?"

More disagreements; this time, they were whispering, and I heard someone in the background say, "This is fucked up, man."

"You'll be fucked up if you don't maintain your mouth!"

The caller was the boss. If Jevaun had not cleared this, I'd have ended the call. I wasn't a fan of team debate.

"We're at the edge of the mountain at the lake," the man stated. "Lots of trees, and it's down the slope. You need to go behind the old school that burned up a few years ago. It used to be a crackhouse before it caught on fire."

I stated that I understood in a manner that the caller thought I was writing down his details.

"Jones Lake. Edge of Cotton Mountain. Down the hill. Travel behind the old Central Reform School – the old, burnt-up dope house."

"Yeah, you're spot on, man."

"Number of individuals?"

"It's, uh, me and," the caller counted, "it's three, four, and . . ."

"OK."

"Wait, wait, wait a minute." There was additional conferring, and the caller put the phone on mute. "Alright, it's five total, but we need you to handle something when you get here."

I did not acknowledge the request other than to ask, "Anything else I need to know?"

"No. We just need you to make moves."

"See you before the end of the hour."

TREPIDATION

I sent three text messages.

Not knowing was always the most complicated part, but being prepared made things easier.

I drove to my storage facility, punched in my code, and moved near the back, where customers boarded their campers and boats. I had three units throughout the city, but this one housed my Chevy Suburban 2500. It was an older version, but it matched the situation and my destination.

Inside the storage unit, I grabbed two small gym bags containing the necessary items for this incident and a snub-nosed revolver, which I strapped to my ankle for insurance.

My Beretta was already comfortable and snug in my shoulder holster. I grabbed some extra supplies, a case of water, and some peanut butter MREs.

When I ran the point, it was always the same crew, including my best friend, Salvatore. I didn't trust many. Jevaun was the liaison for the missions and payments.

For this assignment, Radar sent me four still shots and some live videos of the scene he captured from his drones.

After hearing all the stories, I felt honored to work with Radar. He sent a message saying he'd obtain facial recognition in six minutes or less. From phone taps to launch codes to a nuclear submarine, he was the 'go-to' guy. I never asked how and assumed it was on a need-to-know basis.

Cire Muhammad was a sophisticated Nigerian raised in London. He was all muscle, not to mention a great sharpshooter. He was built like young Mike Tyson but taller; I told him he looked like Xavier McDaniels from the New York Knicks. Cire disagreed and said he resembled Morris Chestnut, except Morris wished he had a body like his.

Salvatore Hudson, better known as Sal or salamander, as he preferred, was my wild card, my Swiss army knife, and my best friend. After our time at the academy, we went on different paths. I was in intelligence operations, but Sal passed everything with high marks and went off the grid after graduation.

I'd receive cards and messages with a picture of a lizard at the bottom, which became his tag. He blended in everywhere - invisible in plain sight. Someone you remembered but could overlook. He looked like your everyday, unsuspecting tenth-grade biology teacher, but retained 42 variations to send you to an untimely burial. I imagined Radar tripled that.

Cire's text message read: "En Route. 6 mins."

Sal leaned against his maroon Dodge Ram. A pile of sunflower seed shells suggested he was waiting longer than I expected. He looked disturbed but in check.

"Cire in the vicinity?"

"En route," I replied and dapped him up, finishing with a fist bump.

Sal sucked his teeth.

"Problems with C?"

Sal sucked his teeth again. "Cire? Hell no! C's my guy. If you didn't know, I'm his favorite wingman. He knows I can hold my own with the ladies. C's my guy. This fucking tea bag broke in my container, so I have all these micro leaves in my water, my cheeks, and my gums, and it's fuckin' driving me nuts. I can't enjoy my tea. Don't worry. I'm dialed in."

"Good. The last thing I need is the crew having issues."

"I thought everything was disco at the house," Sal inquired.

"Meh, it's way better than before, but something's still off. I told Radar to let it go, but ping me if it was an affair. So far, no ping, so no unfaithfulness."

"Or Radar took the target out; no ping was required."

"Really, Sally?"

"Just saying." Sal sucked his teeth. "Radar likes you a lot, Bro, and he handles shit like that without blinking. It's in his DNA."

"This won't solve anything if Alana was fucking around on me."

"Sure, it will. If Radar eliminated the target, then, ya know, no more fucking around," Sal retorted. "If you gave him the green light, Alana would be pfft, too."

I pointed at Sal in response to that nonsense, but my phone buzzed. Radar sent close-ups of the scene. I froze as a massive amount of adrenaline rushed through my body down to my feet. My eyes told the story, and Sal grabbed my phone.

"Oh shit! We have to move now! You good?"

I didn't say anything. I walked to the passenger side of the Suburban and grabbed my rifle. Sal went to the back seat of his Dodge and did the same. We knew Cire already had gear with him.

Radar sent another text: "Sending Tyson." Tyson was Radar's military-grade drone equipped with projectile-launching weapons. The kind that eliminates targets with the mushroom plume. One blow of Tyson, and you're out or worse. I never asked Sal how Radar acquired this multi-million-dollar machine, but he had it.

I told Sal, "Tyson is airborne," but I had new thoughts. Did Jevaun double-cross me?

Was he aware of the people who phoned him and had my daughter, Sara?

What was Sara doing with these people?

Didn't she have swim practice?

Did they touch her?

Was she hurt?

When she left the house for school, I didn't think she'd be involved in something like this by the end of the day. It gave me chills inside to think of losing my only child.

I made it a habit to hug and kiss her forehead before she left the house.

We bonded more in the last few weeks when I thought Alana was cheating on me. I'd pick her up from swim practice and chatted about her techniques, the next meet, and her times. She told me she wanted to visit UCLA. She liked USC but wanted to improve her time or be a state champ. We ate dinner together and even watched a few movies on TV. I don't know how I did it, but my daughter enjoyed '90s hip-hop and shows on AMC and Nick at Nite. I missed today's moment as she left before I woke.

I looked at the pictures from Radar, searching for new clues, scenarios, and strategies. I zoomed in on my daughter to detect any stress or pain. Radar's video only showed the young men talking, but the third time revealed another young lady lying on a tarp or blanket.

I couldn't tell if she was dead or alive: I showed Sal the playback. I knew Cire received the same thing. He was somewhere in the woods - in position – and waiting for my signal. He must have read my mind because my phone vibrated.

"Sara is down there, Chuck."

"I know, C. Whatever we thought this was going to be is different now."

"I got clear shots on everyone except one fella hanging out with the other girl. Sara does not appear to be experiencing any anxiety and is talking freely to two men. I imagine she's doing what Daddy taught her."

I didn't respond. Sal was sucking his teeth again and nodded to let me know he was ready to go. I shot him the Hawaiian "hang loose" sign, and he disappeared in the dusk.

Radar's text popped up over Cire's screen. "Tyson is on STUN and in position."

"Alright, C, maintain your position until we go there. Sal is on his way, and I'm heading down the hill."

"They'll be 100 yards from the top of the hill."

"Copy."

"You know I'll clip them all before they take their next breath, Bruv," Cire reminded me.

"I know, C, but I wanna know what the fuck is going on. Too much shit has been off recently."

"Just say the word."

My approach was complex, with the autumn leaves changing and scattered throughout the ground. They knew I was coming, but I still liked the element of surprise. Each step echoed by the leaves crumbling and crunching underneath my boots. I imagined Sal sucking the tea leaves from his teeth and cussing about the foliage.

My pace was more consistent with the urgency at the mountain basin. As I navigated the dark woods, too many thoughts swirled in my head. I clicked on the night vision feature on the eyeglasses.

My earpiece buzzed. "Dude, what the fuck?"

"What is it, Sal?"

Cire's text message read, "Second woman, Alana."

I changed my stride to a run, navigating through the trees and down the hill, bracing for slight trips by holding on to smaller trees. Branches and twigs swiped my face, and a welt formed on my left cheek. Whatever was happening at this lake now touched my soul.

Not only was my daughter at this deserted location with unfamiliar men, but now my wife is there too?

HYSTERIA

I refrained from activating the drone even though it stood set to stun. I didn't want mishaps or crossfires and needed to know what was happening. I reconsidered carrying my rifle as this sent a different message. I thought I didn't need it, but I was glad I had it.

My team could clip any subject within seconds, but something felt wrong. Unnerving energy filled me. My cheek was bleeding, but I continued to descend the hill.

Sal's transmission in my ear wasn't clear, but I could pick up that he was in position and close to Sara.

Cire said he could clip the man next to Alana with no problem.

I reminded the team that the drone was set on stun, but to keep alert as I approached the scene. I made my appearance obvious by shuffling down the slope to the base of the hill, kicking up the dried, crunching leaves.

One of the men shouted, "There he is," like he was surprised I made it.

I saw Alana first. She was sitting on a blanket, not a tarp, with her knees tucked under her chin. Her brown, curly hair was pulled back into a ponytail. She winked at me to tell me she wasn't hurt and was glad to see me. I nodded to let her know it was all good.

Sara was sitting on the tabletop of a wooden picnic table. She stood to greet me, but the captor guided her back to sit.

"Right on time and at the top of the hour, as you guaranteed."

It was the voice I heard 55 minutes ago.

His voice was calmer than his dramatic speech earlier. He was about three inches taller than me and overdressed in REI gear. He was polished and looked remarkably familiar, but I couldn't place where or when we had met.

"I keep my word, but please explain why these lovely ladies are here with you?"

"Soon. But for now, you can put the rifle down over there, and can you call your two snipers down the hill so no one gets hurt?"

A skinny man wearing just as much hiking gear as his older leader walked over and took the rifle from me. He smelled of cedar and chewed tobacco, and he removed the magazine clip with the ease of a professional. I maintained a straight face as if I were at a poker table with four aces in my hand. I looked around to see what the other two men were doing, but assumed they were just additional chess pieces to gain a competitive advantage.

"So, are you going to ask your buddies to join us or not?"

"I beg your pardon?"

The senior leader walked closer to Sara and played with her hair.

"Let's not play games, my friend. Jevaun informed me you always travel with a guardian angel or two, so let's meet your team. No games, or these lovely ladies will be extremely uncomfortable for the rest of their lives."

I had been in worse situations in graver scenarios, but not when the blueprint was in my opponent's hand.

It was official: Jevaun set me up. But why? Did someone pay him money to eliminate me? Was this a revenge hit? Was I the weak link because I took some time away from the operation? Sal knew my situation. Jevaun knew I was trying to clear my head. No one wants a teammate with the YIPS.

I sent an all-clear code to Cire and Sal, allowing them to meet with me without deliberation. Sal chirped in my ear, "Fuck, man! I don't like this. On my way. Fuck!"

We waited for Sal and Cire to arrive. I studied the man. "Have we met?"

"We have not."

"You sure? I'm pretty good with faces."

He shrugged his shoulders.

"Has anyone ever told you that you look like the Dos Equis guy?"

The man didn't respond.

Cire approached from the left side of the lake, wearing all black and carrying a garment bag.

"Jesus H, he's a big dude," the third man of the group said. His accent reminded me of a former contract from Tennessee.

Alana and I caught each other's glance for a spell. She mouthed something I couldn't make out, then blushed at our private exchange.

Sara yelled, "Hi, C!" She loved saying Hi-C to him because of the drink.

Cire nodded and waved without emotion. Alana stood and kissed him as he approached, "Glad to see you, C."

"You too." He handed her the garment bag, and Alana walked next to our daughter by the picnic table. Cire moved over, patted my left leg, found my ankle holster, and took the .22 out of my pocket.

"Let's talk, Chuck."

I looked at Cire and then at the skinny attendant, attempting to survey the area. It was all unclear.

When we left our vehicles, Sal went down the crunchy hill carrying a duffel bag I didn't recall him having.

"Look, Bruv, don't try to figure this shit out," Cire said, pointing his 9-millimeter at my midsection. "It's too complicated."

"Complicated?" I mustered a fake but nervous laugh. "This shit appears way the fuck outside complicated, man. What the hell is this?"

I turned to face my wife, "Alana, you OK, Babe?"

My wife didn't acknowledge me. She helped Sara off the picnic table. The older man grabbed the duffel from Sal and walked up the hill, looking down at his phone. My recall of faces failed me with this man. Where have I seen him before?

Sara turned and said, "Bye, Daddy. I love you."

"Love you, too, Sweetie. Be careful. I'll see you in a few."

The other collaborators picked up items around the area as if they were cleaning up, leaving no evidence that anyone had been there. The drones hovered eight feet above us. I turned back to Cire with more questions.

"What the fuck is this, C?" I was losing my patience, and no one was saying anything.

"Hold tight."

"Hold tight? How long have we known each other, man? How many missions have we done together? How much fucking money have we made together, Bro? Is this about money, because I can get you all the bread you need? Just let Sara and Alana go, man."

Cire looked at his watch and raised his eyebrows, as if he were doing math. "With respect, it's not about the money, Bruv."

"Then what is this, man? Are you and Alana hooking up? Have you been sleeping with my wife, man? Talk to me, C. Who's behind all of this?"

Cire shook his head, checked his watch, and said nothing but "Radar."

"Radar?" I asked. "What about Radar?"

I never experienced being shot or sprayed with stun pellets from a drone, but the voltage got my attention quickly. I looked at Cire. He placed his hands on my shoulders to hold me up and brace my fall. A few more pellets hit me in the back, and a freezing, electric sensation overwhelmed me, like the tingling feeling after my arm falls asleep, but this was all over my body.

I gazed in the direction where my wife and daughter were before blacking out, but they were gone, and I felt myself fading.

"What……the…. fuck, Cire?"

CONFUSION

I woke up in a moldy, humid room, dizzy and unsure of my surroundings. There was a faint smell of mildew, chlorine, and charcoal burning. The lack of sustenance keyed on charcoal, but I couldn't determine if my brain was rebooting from the stun gun or if I was out of it.

Decorated with black and white tiles, the floor, in its checkerboard style, gave me the impression of a classroom. I was lying on a cot. I wasn't tied up, gagged, or handcuffed, so I reached the large steel door. It didn't match the empty room of my incarceration and was newer than the rest of the confined space. It lacked a handle, and there were no slots for communication or supplies, so my jailer could control their entry.

I leaned against the cold, steel door. My eyes were closed as I pinched the bridge of my nose and pressed the mental playback of what occurred, trying to make sense of this twisted incident. I struggled to resolve the rage forming, thinking Cire and Alana were fucking.

All I remembered at the bottom of the hill was Alana kissing Cire like she had done it before. Did Radar know about this? He was supposed to inform me if Alana was seeing someone. Were he and Cire in cahoots? Did Sal know?

Jevaun set all this in motion with his text message, so Sal had to know, and Radar's drones shot me! Several times! Son of a Bitch!

Nothing made sense to me, but it was starting to come together. Jevaun had not paid us for this assignment yet, and I didn't bother to think about it because he was always good for it.

Now, it was apparent. Sal had a duffel bag large enough to contain payment and a handsome bonus for the rest of the crew for sending me away. The older leader had to be Jevaun's handler or a different contractor. If this was the plan, somehow, they involved my family.

I was in a cell in the woods where no one could find me. A sense of calm overwhelmed me because my wife and daughter were not in danger, which meant whatever was going to happen to me did not impact their suffering. After these covert operations, I was aware of the risks associated with my assignments and missions, and I had prepared Alana many moons ago.

It was first a favor for Jevaun. He and Sal knew each other from an underground operation in Kabul. When they landed at Vandenberg Airport in L.A., Jevaun received multiple messages regarding the disappearance of his niece. It was summer, and Jevaun's niece, Tamika, met a rapper on Instagram. They DM'd each other, chatted on Zoom, and FaceTimed each other for months. She thought she was in love with the rapper J-Rock. She drove to Myrtle Beach to hang out with him while he performed as an opening act at a summer concert series, similar to Coachella. After a few nights, she told the artist she was going back up North, and the rapper said he wanted her to stay longer. He convinced her to return the rental and gave her access to his driver, his key card to his suite, and cash to buy new clothes.

Tamika was smitten. The rapper didn't try anything shady. They spooned in bed and played touchy-feely games at night. In the morning, J-Rock ordered breakfast, and Tamika ate until she was ready to nap.

She felt something wasn't right when the rapper's bodyguard showed up and refused to let her leave the suite. He told her it was for everyone's protection because people could follow her back to the room.

Tamika considered the guard's direction to be legitimate. After all, he'd been on the road with J-Rock, and she knew wanna-be video girls and groupies would find their way to the suite. Yet, things felt off. J-Rock would pick her up from the suite and travel to his trailer before he performed on stage. His bodyguard would direct her back to the trailer when she attempted to accompany the rapper.

After two more days of back-and-forth, Tamika was over the experience from the suite to the trailer and ready to jump out the window. On the third day, J-Rock and his team left while Tamika slept. Other women slept on the couch and chaise lounge when she woke, but no one else was in the suite. She called her uncle Jevaun repeatedly with multiple messages.

Jevaun informed me that he obtained my information from Sal—a reliable source—and that this favor was a matter of life or death. He provided the details, and I made my way to South Carolina. I called in a few favors of my own and received all-access passes. I located J-Rock's hotel and made my way to the suite.

When I approached the door, I detected a man arguing with another man, and the voices of other females sounded like the soprano section of a choir. I wasn't sure if Tamika was among the disputing voices, so I tapped on the door with the key card I obtained from security.

"Housekeeping."

"Yo, housekeeping has already been up here," the bodyguard shouted.

I tapped on the door without ceasing, "Housekeeping." I knew two things. It would piss the protector off when he'd open the door, and I had to be ready when he opened it.

I stepped back, got in a three-point football stance, and waited. When the protector flung the door ajar, I charged and drove my shoulder into his sternum like the all-pro linebacker I dreamed of being. The impact of my collision and my leverage propelled him off his feet as we crashed on the floor. His hot breath escaped his mouth as his spirit departed from his body. *SPLASH!* He was out cold.

"Daaaaayum," the lady vocalized. "Who you?"

I patted the guard for weapons and asked, "Any of you ladies, Tamika?"

One of the women wearing a lime green ruffle trim wrap dress exposing cleavage said, "Shieeeet, I'll change my name to Tamika for your fine ass. You knocked that muthaphuqqah all the way out."

She high-fived another curvy woman in a 'look-at-me' crop top and plaid shorts two sizes too small for her.

Tamika appeared from the other room wearing modest clothes compared to the other three women.

"I'm Tamika."

I extended my hand, "Nice to meet you, Tamika. I'm Chuck, your Uncle Jevaun's associate, and it's time to go."

Jevaun didn't ask how I had located her, and I didn't reveal how I had done it. J-Rock no longer had a hip-hop career and was no longer in the public eye. My account was ten racks healthier, and Jevaun suggested he, Sal, and I set up an operation to help people with particular circumstances. Jevaun's relationship with the CIA allowed him to conduct sensitive operations on US soil without their direct involvement, and we were heavily compensated for our unique cases.

Now, I was in a unique case.

Mid-thought of my infuriated reflections, a cell phone rang underneath the cot. I staggered to the cot to reach for the burner device.

"Hello, Love." It was my wife. "How are you feeling?"

I inhaled and held in my rage. My wife had never given me a reason to be angry with her, but this was a different level.

"Chuck?"

"Alana?"

"Listen, babe, you need..."

"Don't you, 'Babe' me! What the fuck is this? Are you behind all of this?"

My wife snickered, and I could hear her smiling when she answered. "Well, I am, but I had appropriate help."

"Jevaun?' I asked, "Cire?"

"Oh no, Honey, this was Sal's idea. We figured you wouldn't suspect your best friend, for how long have you known Salvatore?"

The restrained fury returned as my traitorous wife's cavalier conversation continued. "I mean, what the fuck is this, Alana? What do you want? What does Sal want?"

There was a pause of deliberation from my new enemy.

"Well, all I want you to do is go to the other room. You'll find your toiletries, so clean yourself up. The shower works, but it heats up, so be careful not to scold yourself. Please take care of the scrape on your cheek. There are some towels and clothes in there for you as well. *Bilisan Mo!*"

Alana disconnected the call after telling me to hurry in her Philippine dialect.

I hit the call button, hoping to call Alana back, but the phone was a one-way device. I didn't notice the vestibule in the corner of my compartment. I only saw the steel door when I woke from my unexpected slumber.

Still loopy from the shock shots, I wobbled to the other room. It was a small bathroom, and I grasped that I was in the old reform school the scraggly leader had told me about earlier. I presumed the charcoal was the source of the charred smell from the burned-out building.

The scent of bleach, a chilled bottle of Gatorade, and an energy bar got my attention. It was a nice touch, and I wondered who thought of the gesture. Was it Alana's peace offering?

I gobbled the energy bar and took massive gulps of the melon-flavored juice until it was gone. It revived my dehydrated body as the coolness traveled down my dry throat to my empty stomach.

The school lavatory and shower were over-sanitized. I looked through the items Alana brought from our house for additional clues, but they were just things to clean up.

A tuxedo hung on the hook, with my black double-monk shoes, sateen socks, and underwear. Was I cleaning up for my funeral?

The water was as red-hot as Alana indicated, and it felt like I was there for over 30 minutes when I heard the burner phone ringing. I grabbed the towel and scooted my wet feet on the slippery tile.

"How's it going, Chuck?" It was not Alana, but it confirmed my earlier feelings.

"What do you want, Jevaun?" I did my best to practice restraint. Everyone was under my wife's influence.

"How long are you going to clean yourself up, dude? We got shit to do."

"We? Who's we, Jevaun? Listen, whatever this is…"

"Look, man," Jevaun interrupted, "dry off, put the suit on, and don't try anything when the door opens. You know we are full of surprises, you know?"

"Jevaun."

The phone disconnected.

I examined the disposal device, searching for answers, and briefly inspected the door. I returned to the temporary dressing room and searched for any surveillance devices, but I soon abandoned that thought.

The team was stellar, and we took pride in our stealth maneuvers. I submitted and dressed in my soon-to-be burial garments. I rubbed my jawline and chin, shaving away the two-day growth. I was extra careful around the abrasion.

I struggled with the shirt's top button and left the collar open - no tie - out of defiance—my middle finger to Alana, Cire, Jevaun, and Sal.

Radar, too, but he was the least conforming to this murder mission. Since Sal repeated the idea, I assumed he respected me as if I were a brother.

I leaned against the countertop, looking directly into the mirror. I studied myself and looked longer to determine if this was a two-way mirror. About eight inches from the mirror, I heard a whooshing sound as the heavy metal door in the other area opened.

"Daddy?"

"Sara!"

I was emotional and ran to her, one shoe on, the other in my hand. I hugged her hard and dropped the shoe. Tears streamed down my face and onto her bare shoulders. She wore a navy blue beaded satin dress I got for her homecoming dance last year.

I remember fussing with her in the middle of Nordstrom's over the price for something she'd barely worn three times before, as the style or her taste had changed. Plus, I told her the dress exposed too much of her body, and I wasn't a fan of too much skin for a teenage girl. This made her fourth since our interaction.

I continued to hold her and sobbed. I told her I loved her and hoped to see her grow into a beautiful woman.

There was much more I wanted to teach her and tell her before she left for college. College will differ from high school, and she'll begin life's next chapter. She'd attend a school on a swimming scholarship, and she might even meet her husband there. I hoped to walk her down the aisle when she got married to someone, someone I wished I liked, and danced with her during the reception. During my toast, I'd threaten to paralyze the guy if he harmed my daughter, but I'd say it in a way everyone knew I was joking - but he'd know I was serious. I wanted to be a Pop-pop and see my granddaughter at a dance recital or my grandson win a chess tournament.

Sara hugged me and became emotional, too.

"Are you hurt, Daddy? This is wild! What is going on?"

"I'm fine, I'm fine," I told her and was surveying her to ensure she was OK, too. "Who are these people, Sara? Where do you know the Dos Equis man from? What happened? How did you and your mother find yourselves at Jones Lake?"

The room was spinning. Sara was talking, but I couldn't hear anything. The spinning increased, and I grabbed my head.

"Daddy, are you okay?"

I wanted to answer, but the room was moving too fast, and I understood my special treat and drink in the bathroom were a sedative of some sort. A Dr. Goyle cocktail. Shit!

"I.... I am.... I'm not sure, Sweetie. I need to sit down over here." I moved towards the makeshift bed, and Sara grabbed my arm.

I slumped onto the cot, almost out of it. I fought for consciousness, hoping Sara would reveal something to me.

She was yelling and shaking me by my shoulders, attempting to keep me conscious, but I could not fight the dosage. Tears streamed down her cheeks.

"Daddy! Daddy, please wake up!"

She was saying something, and I could not comprehend.

EUPHORIA

Dr. Goyle's sedative was powerful. I had a lucid dream of Alana and me living in an obscure apartment. Sara was maybe a couple of months old in this dream and wouldn't stop crying.

Alana complained because her breast reacted to Sara's crying and produced milk, but the baby was full, and Alana grumbled over the pain. We were young in this dream, and I was right out of the academy, so we didn't have any fancy gadgets mothers used to pump. Sara was crying, Alana was cussing, and I walked around in circles, hunting for solutions.

"Do you think she's hungry?" I asked.

"I just fed her, and my tits feel like they will explode. Look at them!" They were extra-extra-large, but it was a dream.

"It's gas. She has to burp or something," I deduced.

"Fed burped and changed, Captain," Alana mocked because I was only a lieutenant.

"Could she be teething? I heard babies cry a lot when their teeth came in."

"She's hardly two months old, Chuck, so she's not teething. Just take her because she obviously doesn't like me and doesn't want anything I have. God, my tits feel like rocks right now."

I took my daughter from my frustrated wife and walked seven steps into the living room, which wasn't bigger than our bedroom.

Sara was crying hard; her face became red, and I thought she had stopped breathing. It was only a second or two, and she belted an angry cry in protest.

"What's going on in there?" Alana inquired.

I returned to the bedroom door and found our daughter crying. I returned to the playboard entertainment center, where an elaborate display of jazz and hip-hop CDs was on display. My imaginative dream selected artists I liked but didn't own.

I pressed play on the carousel CD player, hoping whatever was there would calm Sara. She was losing it.

The first seven or eight notes of Johnny Griffin's "Nice and Easy" commenced, and Sara settled. It was like she searched the room for the new noise and had to discover it. The saxophonist played his song for four minutes. I let Sara know everything was going to be all right.

The music stopped, and Sara began to cry. Another piece came on before she exploded into a full howl, and calm returned.

"So, you like jazz, huh?" I did not expect her to answer. I saw my parents and other adults blabbering to babies, and I believed it was silly. Babies can't talk. I vowed I'd never do such an absurd thing with my child, and found myself doing it in this dream.

"Do you like Wayne Shorter? He is one of the great artists from the Blue Note label. 'Speak No Evil' is the name of this song, and I don't want you to say evil things either. I got you. Daddy's got you."

Sara hushed, looking at me like she understood every word. She was calm, and when Thad Jones' "April in Paris" played, she was asleep in my arms. I kissed her on her forehead.

DISMAY

I recovered from my second collapse on the same day. I woke up refreshed, like after a good night's rest. I didn't know how long I was out, but I knew I was transferred from the mini cell to a comfortable seat with padding on the arms, back, and bottom. I was cloaked with a dark hood and handcuffed to the sides.

I was in a different part of the burned-out jail. It was more confined, and another smell of burning seeped through the hood. I detected movement as someone rattled off football players' names. It sounded like the same man from the woods.

"Staubach, Calvin Hill, Dorsett, Pearson, and Tony Hill from the old school." It was the same voice.

"What about Butch Johnson? Remember him with his touchdown celebrations? The other voice was Sal. Sal was in the room, passing the time with the man from the woods.

"Meh, he was entertaining like Hollywood Henderson, but not one I'd have on my list. Memorable, yes, but not a role player. It's not like he's in the Hall of Famc."

"Alright, who else on the defensive side?" Sal asked the voice.

"Deion Sanders, Demarcus Ware, Too Tall Jones, and Randy White get love in my book, Everson Walls, Dennis 'Hitman' Thurman, and Charles Haley. Haley was a monster."

"No one could stop Haley, you're right. Those are some good ones," Sal said and chuckled. "Funny, you mentioned Everson Walls. I used to date this babe who was his cousin or his niece or something."

"No shit?"

"I shit you not," Sal retorted to the familiar voice. "I was double-dating with C as his wingman, and he had a smoker, but I've never seen C with anyone less than nine. Eight point nine-nine if she's got a bad attitude, ya know?"

The two men laughed.

"Anyway, C introduces me to his date and the other gal," Sal continues. She was cute, but a little too short for my taste. However, she had all the other essentials I like, making up for it. From what I can recall, she has a unique name: Elaine or Tremaine, no, Elaine.

"So, I'm sitting there making small talk with Elaine, and I say, 'Tell me something unique about yourself,' because it's my way of remembering something about people I meet, and she asks me if I like football.

"I remember saying, 'What straight, warm-blooded American man doesn't like football?" Sal said. "Of course, I like football. What about it? She goes, 'I'm related to Everson Walls."

"No shit?"

"Yeah, man," Sal responded. "No shit. She was good people. I liked her. Quiet but fun to hang out with. I did most of the talking and brought up things to discuss. We were an item for a little while. You know how it goes. Dinner dates, comedy shows, plays, cooking dinner for each other, going to top-notch restaurants, a few soul food spots, some jazz sets, and even some greasy spoon joints on the avenue to mix it up a little. It was the real deal. We even took a trip to Catalina Island for an extended weekend. That place is a hidden gem if you ask me, and our courtship lasted longer than Cire did with the other gal, but we're talking about C here."

"C shuffles them like a card deck, and they're all winning hands, in my opinion," the voice said. "It sounds like you didn't pull any punches. Whatever happened to Elaine Walls? I assumed it was her last name, too?"

Sal said, "Yeah, Walls was her last name. Yeah, she was a special lady. She wanted to be a dentist or something in the medical field. She joined the army, and we lost contact. I could have kept an eye on her and even made some ties if it was real, but she was too short for my taste."

The voice asked, "Wait. You specifically said it was the real deal, but you lost interest in this young queen because she was too short?"

"Pfft. It was real for me at the time," Sal countered. "As I said, she was fun but too short for my taste."

"You have more taste buds than a catfish," I said, letting everyone in the room know I was alive and conscious.

The door opened and closed, and someone said something to Sal's companion. The stranger acknowledged the third party and said it was okay to stick around. The new voice asked me if I was OK. I didn't recognize this unfamiliar person's voice, but she was younger.

I perceived Victoria's Secret fragrance from the young lady. Sara wore the same perfume.

"Let me guess," I said. "Coconut Passion."

"It is my favorite," the female voice responded.

"Enough," Sal stopped my chat with the young lady. He was close enough to me that I could smell roasted pecans on his breath through my hood. "You could get yourself ten to twenty years in some states, buddy. Tread lightly."

"How long will this dance last, Salvatore?" I asked.

"Oh, we're getting formal now, Chuck," Sal quipped. "No longer 'Sal' only after a few hours? The song and dance have not commenced yet, but will *soon come,* as our island brethren, Jevaun says. I'm waiting for Alana to give me a call."

I had to ask.

"So, Alana is pulling all the strings on this, not you?"

Sal and the two strangers in the room snickered.

"I'm smart, buddy, but I needed a decoy. Your wife was the perfect pawn. You were moping around about her having some new meat. I mean, I got several tricks up my sleeve based on all our little capers, but this, by far, is genius. This is something for the books; we'll all laugh at your expense. Remember, a good player knows his capabilities and limitations and combines them with his skills, ya know?"

I tugged at the restraints, hoping the arms were weak enough to break. I yanked, pulling my arms to launch out of the chair in agony, frustration, and despair.

"Just do it, Sal!" I yelled. "Just fucking put a bullet in my head, man! Fucking do it!"

"Hey, hey, hey, language," the voice barked. "There's a young lady in the room.'

"You want me to do it?" Sal asked. "Like right now?"

"Yeah, man. End it. Whatever this is, just end it. I can't. I can't, man."

I sobbed, which was more challenging than it had been earlier with Sara, because this cry reminded me of the tears I had shed on Sara's shoulder. The shoulder I'd see no more.

"Just fucking do it, man," I cried out.

"Language!" The football fan reminded me. He told Sal, "He's ready. Do it."

Sal cleared his throat and sucked his teeth like he was getting those tea leaves out of his teeth again. "Pretty lady, you wanna leave us alone; we're all set here."

The young lady acknowledged Sal and left the room.

Sal walked between my legs, his hands on my knees. He'd straddle me like a gentleman's club dancer if he were any closer.

"This is what's going to happen, buddy," Sal directed. "I, oh, and my good friend here are going to load ya up on a dolly, and we're going to push you to the next room where we can put you out of your misery. Don't try anything stupid because I will, I promise, I will put a knife through your ear to your skull. Then your daughter. Are we clear, Charles? Since we're getting all formal and shit."

My mind was moving, and the neurons were firing off multiple scenarios. This was a good plan. The remnants of the stun pellets, the somnolent cocktail, and adrenaline overwhelmed me. I was hyperventilating as the two men hoisted me on a flat dolly and rolled me through a corridor.

"Leave Sara out of this," I cried, "just fucking do it, Sal!"

"Shut the fuck up, man," the other voice ordered as they guided me through some lefts and rights, bumping against the walls and corners of the hallways. "No one's going to bother your kid."

We stopped momentarily, and Sal directed the other gentleman inside to ensure Alana was ready. The man left, and Sal assumed his previous position with his hands on my knees.

He took a deep breath and held it for a moment. As he exhaled slowly, he said, "This is it, doc."

"Whatever, Sal; I'll see your punkass in the afterlife."

Sal laughed heartily, slapping my knees harder than I expected. "Famous last words," Sal jested. "You're fucking hilarious, bro! The afterlife? You're too much, Bro!"

"Whatever, man, and I'm not your bro!"

The doors swooshed open, and I thought several people were within my peripheral vision. I smelled chlorine again. Did the school have a pool? The stranger returned to help Sal push me. My hunch was correct, as I heard whispers, quips, and giggling. There were additional people in this room, and it sounded like waves.

"Careful over there, fellas," I heard Jevaun say. Jevaun was in the room and asked Sal if he needed any help.

"Yeah, help me push this bastard up this ramp," Sal said.

"How ya doing, you sonofabitch?" Jevaun said, squeezing both sides of my neck, as if applying the Vulcan pinch. I closed my eyes but did not wince or cry aloud to escape the pain.

I didn't relish giving any famous last words for people to repeat when I was dead, so I remained quiet. We were beyond the ramp and on a landing of some sort. There was a lot of give, like a diving board. What the hell? The men lifted me off the dolly and pushed me onto the platform.

"Don't uncuff him yet," Alana said.

Was she going to be the one who killed me? Is this why she disappeared in the mornings? Using Sal to do temp checks with me at the wing spot?

Alana walked over to me and whispered something to me. I couldn't understand, so Alana addressed the area. Her voice echoed throughout the room.

"I remember my aunt used to read me a Persian poem from Omar Khayyam, '*Ah, make the most of what we yet may spend before we too descend into the Dust descend.*' Chuck, I hope you feel you lived your life to the fullest."

Sara approached me. "Hi, Daddy," she said apprehensively. "Do you promise not to try anything after I uncuff you?"

Tears welled in my eyes. Again. She was indeed my weakness, my kryptonite. "I wouldn't hurt a fiber on you, my love."

She uncuffed my left hand first. I turned my wrist clockwise and counterclockwise to get the circulation going. Before she could uncuff my right hand, someone pushed me backward.

SPLASH!

I sank to the bottom of the pool. I snatched the hood off my head underwater and used my legs to kick the chair's arm from the body. My hand was attached to the chair as I struggled to breathe. I swam to the surface, unsure if Jevaun, Cire, or Sal would be waiting to put a bullet in my head, so I found refuge underneath the diving platform. As I emerged, I yelled out but encountered louder screams and cheers.

"SURPRISE!"

My closest friends, family members, and cohorts dressed in after-five and formal gear stood below the platform with streamers, twirlers, and sparklers. I saw my younger brother, Robbie, in his favorite blue Indochino 2-button tux. I only saw Robbie on special occasions.

"HAPPY BIRTHDAY, CHUCK," was spelled out in gold balloons in a makeshift scaffolding.

Sal helped me out of the pool to embrace me. "Happy Birthday, brother!"

"Man, I don't know if I should be happy or pissed at you."

"Shit got real, huh, champ?"

"Too real."

Sara ran to me, draped me with two large towels, and kissed me. Jevaun handed me another towel and hugged me.

"Happy Birthday, mon! This was harder to organize than any of our missions."

I play-punched Jevaun in the chest and told him, "I always knew you had something to do with all this. It's not how I imagined my birthday, but this was a wild ride. I appreciate you guys."

Cire approached, hand-in-hand with a woman who bore a striking resemblance to Ana Paula Araujo, exuding effortless elegance. I imagined she spoke French or Portuguese.

He was dressed sharp, his dark Bonobos suit hanging just right, casual enough for the night yet perfectly tailored. He gave me a fist bump, then slipped a thick envelope into the pocket of my soaked tuxedo. It felt heavy, stuffed with Benjamins.

"For your troubles, stress, and struggles, and - of course - your birthday, Bruv," Cire said, bowing to me.

I felt mist in my eyes, and my chest tightened from the brotherhood and camaraderie as the older gentleman from the woods approached me.

He wore a gray tuxedo and a Dallas Cowboys lapel pin. As he came, he was with a young woman, my daughter's age.

I squinted to focus. He was the man from the woods, but I knew I'd seen him before. There was some familiarity about him.

He stood before me, waiting for me to figure it out.

"I know you from somewhere."

He looked past me at Sal, and they laughed like they were two bullies teasing my third-grade self at recess.

"Alright, frickin spill it," I demanded.

Sal walked over to the man. Cire and Jevaun joined.

"Look at his face, Chuck."

"I've been looking at him, man. I've been looking at him since I saw him in the woods. Where do I know you from?"

The older man smiled.

"Damn, Chuck, did Dr. Goyle spike the punch too much?" Jevaun asked.

I shook my head as the older man asked for the microphone and held up his glass. There was something about the way he held the glass that triggered my memory.

"A toast!" he declared. The rest of the partygoers held up champagne flutes on cue. "To the man who likes sports bars and hot wings as much as I do. To the brother I never had. I hope you were surprised. Happy birthday, my friend."

Radar!

I bent over, laughed in disbelief, and rested my hands on my soaked pants. Radar sat beside me, watching American Ninja Warrior at the sports bar months ago. He practically participated in the conversation with Sal and me, an unassuming chameleon.

I gave him a high five. I met his niece from the other room. I shook her hand, and Radar gave me a big bear hug.

"It's good to meet you for real, Radar, finally. You are a true shaman," I said during our embrace.

"The pleasure is all mine, brother," Radar said. He pulled me closer and whispered into my ear. "And I took care of that situation involving your wife. That bastard is chopped up and scattered like confetti in three different states. His place looks like he moved out, so no one will be looking for him around here. Consider it an extra birthday gift."

We broke our embrace. My skin wriggled like someone dumped a thousand ants on me. Chilly from the pool, I wrapped the towels tighter and searched the room for Alana. A man dressed in black stood next to the bleachers, waiting for me to notice him. I eyed him like I analyzed Radar in the woods. His gaze pierced a hole in my head, and I knew he was not on the guest list.

Disoriented from the pool, the birthday surprise, Radar's new information about my wife, and now this stranger, I turned to find Alana. She was chatting with our neighbor. She smiled, waved, and blew a kiss in my direction. Eyes watering, I nodded with a smile, then a kissing gesture.

With my head buzzing and feeling like a boulder had landed on me, I looked at Sal. He shot me a grim expression, nodding his head, and I knew it was true.

Splash!

I returned to Radar. "Ray, who's the Colombian by the bleachers?"

Radar squinted over my shoulder, "What Colombian?"

PART II

INCREDULOUS

The ride home could not have been more precise and unbelievably awkward. Sara and Alana laughed, squealed, and teased me about how they had tricked me, surprised me, and gotten me for my birthday. At one point throughout the madness, I forgot it was my birthday. Somebody meticulously plotted everything about this party, from Radar's initial scripted call to me submerging in a pool.

"Did you know Uncle Rob didn't know I was all-conference, Daddy?" I heard Sara's voice but didn't trust myself to respond. "He's staying until next week, Dad. Dad? Daddy!"

Lost in thought, deep thought, more profound than the pool I climbed from. My mind raced a thousand miles a minute, piecing together the dubious pieces of Alana's adulterous secret while preparing a party for me. What kind of psychopath could compartmentalize planning an event and fucking around with her husband? It was ridiculous to ponder as I gazed beyond the passing lane lines. Alana tapped my forearm, which broke my trance. I looked over at the new stranger.

"Your daughter's talking to you," she said between her clenched teeth.

My eyes rose to the rearview mirror and caught Sara's piercing pupils. She never liked being ignored. Even as a high schooler, she still managed to maintain the only-child syndrome. To my defense, my head was still foggy, but I gathered my thoughts, relaxed, and responded.

"Sorry, Sweetie. I'm drained and overwhelmed by tonight's events. What did you say?"

"Uncle Rob did not know I was all-conference."

"That's about to be all-state, right?" Alana startled me with a pinch above my knee. "Don't put that kind of pressure on her, Chuck," my wife interjected, turning to face our daughter.

"Do your best, honey. We're proud of you no matter what, and I think it's special that Uncle Robbie is staying a few days to see you swim. He rarely travels to the supermarket, let alone to another state."

Sara and I met eyes again. She and I knew her mom was full of shit. Sara didn't know what I learned about why Alana missed most of her meets, but she knew her mother wasn't around. Her comment was more a result of guilt than a defense of her daughter. I failed to comprehend that my brother was staying to see his niece swim. Anger was crawling around my neck, squeezing me like a boa constrictor. The anxiety of being less than two feet away from my cheater-of-a-wife overtook my focus not to crash. Bitch.

I chuckled, wondering if Alana knew her lover sprinkled the atmosphere like pollen. If Radar were as meticulous as the rumors, no one would find her cheating accomplice.

I laughed under my breath as this imperfect scenario played out longer than I imagined. Alana casually, comfortably sat shotgun like she was the sweet, innocent, caring mother and wife who gave her husband the best birthday surprise, but I had a surprise for her ass too!

FRENETIC

We pulled into our driveway and waited for the garage door to open. I tapped the mechanism on the sun visor to activate the door. It gaped at a foot and lowered. I hit the button a second time only to experience the same result. I tapped a third time. Nothing. I held my thumb harder, triggering the sensor to reset and open, but to no avail. I clicked the button multiple times out of desperation, but the door didn't open.

"That's bizarre," Alana quipped.

"Daddy, maybe you're pressing it too many times," Sara said.

"Sara, baby, it's been a long, long day, and the last thing Dad wants to do is delay getting in my bed."

"Try it again, Honey," Alana suggested.

I inhaled and let out three little breaths before pressing the button for a sixth time. The door opened and began to rise.

"Bravo," Alana celebrated.

As the door folded, it buckled and jammed. I was perplexed by the door's activity. Then, it jerked and snapped into a million pieces, firing a conglomerate of fiberglass toward our SUV.

"Oh, my goodness!" We all shouted like scary movie-goers. The right side of the door's guardrail bent forward. The springs and coil box flew out, causing the left side to slide off the brace drop, and the body crashed onto the pavement with it.

"Oh, shit!" Sara screamed. Alana covered her eyes, shrieking, "What is it? Oh, my God, oh, my God, what is it? What is it?"

I threw the SUV in reverse and sped away from the house. I punched Sal's code into my phone and rang his number on speed dial.

"Couldn't get enough of me, huh?" Sal joked.

I calmly spewed two words, and Sal knew this wasn't a laughing matter.

"Black beans."

"I'll meet you at the plaza."

I raced through the boulevard, streets, and avenues, glancing for vehicles tailing us, but I didn't notice anyone.

"Daddy, what does baked beans mean?"

"Let your father drive, honey," Alana said. "We're going somewhere safe."

STUNNED

The term "hiding in plain sight" described one of the safehouses we called "Black Beans." We agreed to name the safehouse "Black Beans" when Sal first tasted a savory Jamaican jerk chicken dish with black beans on the side. That night, he ate his dish and anyone else with black beans.

Black Beans was in the heart of downtown, in the center of a gated condominium community. The entertainment district enveloped the condo unit with boutique sushi bars, gourmet restaurants, dance clubs, an all-night bowling alley, and an outdoor roller rink that converted into an ice-skating rink during the holidays. Artsy-fartsy people, doctors, professors, and lawyers lived in this quiet community, even though all the commotion lived outside the perimeter.

The condo's garage door was already open. Sal stood at the foot of the entrance, holding his favorite nine-millimeter. Jevaun was in the background, gripping a double-action Barracuda. He possessed the scariest weapon among us.

"This is totally a different vibe from your birthday party," Sara mentioned.

"I know, Sweetie, but this is for your protection."

"Where's C?" Alana inquired.

"No doubt en route to our house, averting nosy neighbors and, more importantly, the authorities."

Alana buried her face in her palms, "This is insane."

"C'mon," I ordered. "Let's get you two inside so I can return to the house."

"You can't go back, Daddy, it's too dangerous."

"Sara's right," Alana chimed in and held me. "Let your guys handle this one and stay with us." Alana hugged my neck, and I almost forgot she cheated on me.

"It's our house, Alana. I'll be fine. Plus, C's already posted up there or somewhere around there. You're perfectly safe with Jevaun and Sal. I've got some additional guys in stealth mode. No one knows you're here."

Alana gazed at me with her pouty face, but knew it wouldn't work. "Come on, Sara Bear, the sooner your daddy leaves, the sooner he'll return."

"Please be careful, Daddy." I bent down and kissed her forehead, and she hugged my neck harder than her mother. My phone chimed. It was Cire. I read the message and nodded to Sal. He shot me the peace sign.

"I'll be back soon."

I scrambled through the streets and darted as fast as possible on the highway. I doubted anyone was following us, but if they were, I was sure they wouldn't want the smoke waiting for them at the condo.

Cire's text indicated he would meet at the CVS, a half-mile from my house. When I pulled up, he and my neighbor Phil were chatting. Phil was the unofficial neighborhood watchman, and Cire's annoyed expression told me all I needed to know. Phil called 911.

"Holy Christ, Chuck, I thought that was your body lying there." His voice was anxious as he nervously smoked a cigarette. He wore blue Duke Blue Devil basketball shorts, black Nike slides, and a white t-shirt. "I thought someone ran into you, especially when I couldn't make out the speeding car."

"And I take it you called it in instead of calling me?"

Phil froze. "Oh, shit. I screwed up, didn't I, Chuck?"

"We discussed this a hundred times, Phil," I lectured. "Call me first, no matter what."

"Dude, there was a fucking body lying there, and I thought it was you. Hell, the guy looked just like you!"

"Oh, shit, Bruv," Cire chimed in. "Where's Robbie?"

My head spun, and my insides capsized. I heaved up my birthday dinner behind the car. I scrambled, jamming my hand in my pocket to get my phone. I called my brother's number. It rang four times, and a distinct, offshore voice answered, and it wasn't Robbie.

"Bom Dia"

"Who the fuck is this?"

The man snickered. "Who do you want it to be?" He spoke in a Paisan dialect and used a Central or South American greeting.

"Where's my brother?"

"Robbie no here, Pacero."

Furious and sad, I asked again, "Where. Is. My. Brother?"

"Robbie? Robbie, no mas, puta," the man conveyed. I could hear his smirk.

"Look, man, whatever you want, just tell me."

"It was supposed to be you, Chuck, but I'll get you. See ya around, puta." The call disconnected.

I couldn't move. I wondered if this was the man I saw behind the bleachers. I was staring at nothingness when Cire took the phone from me.

"Let me get this number to Radar to trace your bruv's cell."

I dropped to my knees and buried my face in my hands. "Oh, God, no! Not Robbie! Not my brother, man!"

DEVASTATED

Yellow tape decorated the front of my house: two unmarked vehicles, a city patrol car, and a crime scene camper were parked at my dwelling. A unique, windowless SUV was also present, giving me every reason to believe it was the coroner's vehicle. My chest tightened, and my steps lengthened when I recognized one of the detectives. Additional law enforcement members were taking notes and securing the area.

As I approached my house, I recognized Detective Gene Cravis. Cravis reminded me of Sam Jackson's Nick Fury body double. Maybe it was the combination of his black beanie and full goatee. His wire-framed glasses helped as well. He shook my hand and patted me on the shoulder.

"I don't know how to tell you this, Chuck, but"

"I already know, Gene," I interrupted. "I took Alana and Sara somewhere safe and returned to handle the details."

"Any idea what might have happened here?" I shook my head, not revealing the conversation with my brother's murderer.

"We came home from my birthday party, and when I attempted to open the door, it just, just exploded, and a body crashed to the ground. I didn't know if anyone else was in the garage or the house, so I protected my girls and sped off."

The detective scribbled on his pad, capturing my words and observations, which would mold and shape his case. He pulled out a tin can of strawberry Altoids mints and plucked a couple in his mouth. He offered. I shook my head.

He scribbled more notes, looked at other houses, and returned to mine. He'd tell his grandchildren how this case consumed and overwhelmed him, to the point of dyeing his hair to prevent appearing older.

"Happy birthday, despite, you know."

"Thanks, Gene. I get it."

Gene adjusted his hat. He was prepping for additional questions when a young woman dressed in police coveralls approached us. She was young in stature and appeared to be someone who would do this kind of work for free.

"I see you have cameras around your home, but they don't appear to be standard commercial cameras. Are these military-issued cameras?"

My eyes met Gene's; he raised his hand and shook his head in disbelief.

"Tina, Chuck is who we like to say, 'off the books.' We will find what we're looking for from his cameras. Deciphering the footage will provide more evidence than chastising him. He just lost his brother."

Her puppy dog eyes met mine. She adjusted her bob haircut and cleared her throat. "My apologies and condolences, sir."

After a deep breath, I shook my head and asked Gene, "Where is Robbie?"

Gene motioned with his head. We walked over to the van. The detective took a beat and placed his hand on my shoulder again.

"Chuck, it is not pretty. I've got some guys canvassing the area, but I'll also need to send Tina and some others through your house. We can check to see if anything's missing and look at the footage."

"Of course."

The detective grabbed the van's door. He took a moment and turned to me.

"I know you're a fixer, Chuck. I know you. I also know you and your team will do what you must to find this perpetrator."

"Murderer," I interjected.

"Right. I want to do my job too, Chuck. That's all I'm saying. I know you're good people, so if this is a result of you fixing something and someone's coming after you, let me help you. But trussme, I don't need the extra overtime."

The detective stalled to ease my grief and warned me not to play Petey Payback. Either way, I grew more frustrated.

"By the look of that BMW M40 over there, you need all the OT you can get."

Gene chuckled, pointing at the pearl luxury truck. "That? It's my lady's ride. Consider me the lucky man of a former NFL player's wife."

"Congratulations. Can I see my brother now?"

Gene shook his head.

"Detective, do what you want with the paperwork. I don't think it's necessary to identify the body 30 miles away from my house. Just unzip the bag and let me see Robbie."

"Alright, Chuck. We'll do it your way, but remember what I said. I don't want body bags throughout my city."

The detective asked Tina to get back in the van to slide the body out. She changed her black nitrile gloves and unzipped the bag. I folded my arms to brace my emotions.

Robbie was still in his blue Indochino tux. The satin shirt and the jacket trim were blood-soaked as if he were dipped in a bloody fondue dish. Two puncture holes were beneath his right ear, and the bastard caved in my brother's right temple.

I felt like throwing up, but the anguish kept the nausea down. My chest tightened, but I couldn't expand. My eyes burned but wouldn't tear up, though I could hear the air escaping from my nostrils. I bowed my head and said a silent prayer for my brother and our deceased parents. I don't know how long I was in my trance. The detective tapped me on the shoulder.

"Is this your brother, Chuck?" I shook my head. "OK, Tina, please make note that the victim has been identified at the crime scene, and we won't need to contact next of kin."

Tina zipped Robbie back up and slid him back into the van. She motioned to one of her peers dressed in identical garb, and he drove off with my brother. Gene patted my shoulder again as we walked toward the house.

"How'd you two meet?"

"Excuse me?"

"The ex of the NFL player," I said. "How did you two meet?"

"I was called in to investigate a Paint and Sip party gone awry."

"No way! I thought that shit was just for the TV shows."

Gene laughed. "They gotta get their ideas from somewhere."

EXASPERATED

By the time the last set of investigators left my living room, the sun was teasing the day with its morning presence. I ordered donuts, bagels, pastries, hot chocolate, and coffee to express my appreciation and keep them corralled in one area.

I was able to cast the playback of my security cameras to the living room TV using my laptop, and I confirmed the Colombian by the bleachers at my party was, indeed, the man who came to the house to kill me and my family.

I played, rewound, paused, and replayed the footage for what seemed like two hours. Gene inquired countless times if I recognized the man. I said no, but took screenshots and emailed Radar while the police thanked me for the donuts.

I watched the Colombian intruder ambush my brother 15 more times after the police left. My heart rate increased as the stranger applied a rear-naked chokehold on my helpless sibling. This man was a trained assassin with jiu-jitsu skills. Robbie never had a chance.

He approached my house from the left. I hacked three neighbors' security devices to obtain multiple angles of my street. I pulled the footage from two houses away and captured a black Lincoln Navigator letting him out. I sent the plate numbers to Radar, knowing he'd come up with a fake, but it was worth a shot. Did the killer call an Uber? Perhaps he had a team. Maybe the Navi wasn't an Uber.

I played my nosy neighbor Phil's footage and yelled, "Oh shit!" I stopped the playback and grabbed my Beretta M9. The Navigator drove past the house just as the police left my home.

I punched Cire's number.

"Wa Gwaan, Bruv?"

"Are you close?" I asked.

"Always close, Bruv," Cire responded.

"Make sure you're hot."

"Always, Bruv. Slow feet don't eat."

Cire arrived in two minutes.

I pointed at the TV screen to show Cire the black Navigator.

"Rasclot! This is a badman, Bruv. He's one bold mother."

"More importantly, he is sticking around to complete his assignment."

"Well, that's not happening, Bruv," Cire affirmed. "He will be down before that."

On cue, Sal called. I put him on speaker just in case Cire needed whatever information he conveyed.

"Are you sitting down?" I stood up, "What's up, brother? How are the girls doing?"

Sal sighed in my ear. "Well, your favorite detective just called Alana."

"Gene?"

"Of course, genius, who else? Yes, Gene, and he sounded official."

"What did he want?"

"He wants to stop by the house."

My face twisted as if I smelled burnt popcorn. "He was just here."

"I know, I know," Sal retorted. "He told Alana she could come in to talk, or he'd meet her at the house. Considering your spot is still a designated crime scene, he provided options, but...."

When Sal paused, I knew it wasn't good. "It's been a long night, Sallie, spit it out."

Sal sighed again. "He wants Alana to come in and answer some questions about her missing coworker."

Splash.

"You there?"

"Yeah, Sal, I'm here. Take her to the station. I'll have Cire drop me off."

"You sure about this?" Sal inquired. Too much was happening, and my mind was still racing over my brother and stalker. Whether it was the right decision or not, I made the call.

"I think I'm going to use this chat with Gene to get to the bottom of Alana's shit, so yeah, I am very sure. After all, she still doesn't know I know."

Sal laughed. "I'm glad I'm not on speaker."

"You're never on speaker. See you in a few."

DISTRACTED

Cire got me to the police station in less than 15 minutes, when it should have taken us thirty. Alana and Sal were approaching the steps as we pulled up. I closed the car door and tapped my right pec twice. He leaned over the passenger-side window.

"You good, Bruv?"

"Yeah, man," I lied. I was exhausted, and it was catching up with me. "Stay close."

"All the time."

Sal looked perplexed. We did our customary fist-bump routine, and I hugged my wife. She held me longer than I expected and kissed me as we separated our embrace. She nodded over to Sal.

"I'm not sure what this is about, but this guy has more drama than a Tyler Perry movie."

I looked at my friend. Other than his transitioning five o'clock shadow to eight-thirty, he looked OK, but I inquired, "What's up, Sallie?"

"The usual," he spat. "The ones I like, I can't have. The ones that like me, I don't want."

I folded my arms and sighed, "Oh, Sal. You gotta start dating women your age, bro."

"Can we focus on why we're in front of this police station instead of my choice of women? It's the last time I've shared anything with you, Alana."

My wife laughed, "You promise?"

We approached the glass panel and waited for someone to acknowledge us. Two police officers were typing on laptops just beyond the window, and a third walked past us as if we weren't there. Sal's fist was about to hit the panel when Alana tapped his shoulder and shook her head, motherly.

Sal turned to me and Alana in disgust. "You know they can see us, right? I know I'm light brown, but where's the respect for the diaspora?"

"I'll text Gene and let him know we're here."

Sal danced to the 80s music in front of the panel.

"Y'all remember the Roger Rabbit?"

Alana laughed, "I can't with your friends, Chuck, especially this one."

"They don't make 'em like Salvatore anymore."

The door buzzed, and Gene walked out, looking at Sal, who continued to dance, and then at us.

"Is he always like this?"

"Only in police stations," I retorted. "What's up, Detective? Twice in less than eight hours. Did you sleep?"

Detective Cravis didn't answer but used his lanyard to buzz us through the door. He left Sal in the lobby, dancing to a B.T. Express song.

The detective offered Alana and me bottled water. He sat, shuffling papers as he searched for a particular file. I was confident he was tired from the evening. Robbie's file sat on the right side of his desk. He saw me eyeing it and apologized before placing it in his desk drawer.

"Alana, it's been a helluva night for your family, so I won't keep you. It's just formality."

"Sure, Gene," my wife responded. "What's this concerning?"

The detective grabbed his thermos, took a few gulps, put the cap back on, and exhaled his coffee breath. He didn't mean it. He was just tired.

He leaned forward as if he were going to tell us a secret: "Your co-worker Julius Givens is missing, and your colleagues mentioned you were the last one he was seen with, so do you have any idea what may have happened to him?"

I searched Alana's face for reactions, just as the detective did.

"JG's missing?" Alana asked.

"JG?" You call him 'JG,'" I inquired.

"Yeah, is something wrong with that?" Alana snapped. "Everyone in the office calls him JG."

The detective sensed tension and interrupted. "I can ask the questions, Chuck, if you don't mind."

"His family is concerned, and when your vehicle appeared on his Ring camera, we're just curious if you know what happened to him."

I grabbed Alana's chair to face me. "You've been to this dude's house?"

Gene stood, "Easy, Chuck, or I must ask you to step outside. You're here as a courtesy with everything happening."

I stood to meet Gene, "You're right. With everything going on, I need to know what the fuck is going on, so answer the detective's questions, Alana."

Alana took a swig of water. She closed her eyes, placed her palms on her lap, and inhaled as if she were escaping the detective's office. Gene and I sat down and studied my wife. She did a few breathing exercises and opened her eyes. Her initial focus was on me.

"JG's in some kind of danger and thought he was being followed," Alana said. "He mentioned it a couple of times in the office, and we thought he was just being facetious, joking around, but the third or fourth day, he said he wanted to leave his car at the office and asked me to give him a ride home. He's a smart guy, but not street smart, you know? He could have taken a Lyft, but I thought I was being helpful."

Gene pecked on his laptop and looked up, "Please continue, Alana."

"I should have come to you about this," Alana told me. I studied her more. She turned to the detective and continued.

"JG is our IT guy. He works on desktops, PCs, and laptops as a hobby, like a side hustle," my wife explained. "He's a wiz with this stuff, like guys who can take an engine apart and rebuild it blindfolded.

"Anyway, he was working on a city official's personal laptop, and a program opened. He thought he was looking at budget stuff, like for the fiscal year."

"Go on," Gene instructed.

"Well," Alana took another swig of her water. "It was budget stuff, but on another tab, there was money that was associated with fentanyl, methamphetamine, firearms, and other illegal substances. A lot of money."

Gene suggested, "Depending on whose laptop he had, it could have been task force intel."

Alana shook her head. "I don't think so, Gene. It was Mayor Abido's laptop, and some other agency names were listed next to the addresses of where the drugs were located, coming from, or going to. When I gave JG a ride home, he told me what he found, and he was leaving town. He was paranoid. Whatever he found, the mayor must have learned about it."

Gene leaned back in his chair. Rubbing his chin, he contemplated his next thought. He looked at me with a side-eye and cleared his throat.

"I work homicide and missing persons, which usually leads to homicide," he explained. "But the entire station would know about a major bust with that kind of weight."

Alana continued, "As much as I know about Mayor Abido, he's eager to be on TV, social media, or even in the paper."

"Especially when it involves his task force," the detective interjected. "So, Julius Givens isn't technically missing; is that what you're telling me?"

Alana shook her head. "He's hiding, and before you ask, he didn't tell me where he was going."

Gene thanked us for coming in despite our current circumstances with my brother. More questions swirled in my head. Why did Radar lead me to believe my wife was screwing JG?

When we walked to the lobby, Sal was sashaying to Anita Baker's "No One in the World."

"You're going to need a long talk with him," my wife said.

BURGOMASTER

He was deemed a child prodigy at the age of 9, entering high school and graduating before his 13th birthday. He double majored in Political Science and Linguistics, studying and learning French, Spanish, Portuguese, Tagalog, and a little Malay.

Foreign services attracted him, and he earned a foreign affairs fellowship, allowing him to see the world and serve as a Teaching Assistant teaching English in a Yoruban village.

By his 18th birthday, Jefferson Abido was strategizing with US embassies and consulates to design and implement English language programs and resources worldwide. He was a natural bridge builder and a key decision-maker, supporting missions for the United States. He was fast-tracked to take over the office of English Language Programs. Then, his satellite phone rang.

"You have to come home, my son," his mother pleaded. "It's your brother."

"What?"

Across the continents, Jefferson's mom sobbed through the phone line, "Charleston is in a bad way. He was beaten, Jeffy. Those terrible people beat up my Charleston. Real bad."

Although not a prodigy like his younger brother, Jefferson's brother possessed gifted abilities and applied his smarts and ingenuity to other employment opportunities.

His exceptional talents could have led him to any major corporate enterprise, whether legitimate or illicit, but he chose the more unconventional side of life. Charleston's beautiful mind worked mathematical problems like someone would busy themself with a crossword puzzle.

He became adept at counting numbers in gambling houses, analyzing the daily take, and running errands. He was also promoted to comptroller for a local mob family. The Cyphus brothers ran a well-oiled organization that included sports betting, transportation, and sanitation throughout the city. It looked legit on the outside, but those who knew didn't speak of this syndicate.

Charleston's ambition led him down an even darker path when he created a cyberbug in the criminal enterprise, allowing him to misappropriate funds into an offshore account in his brother's name.

The Cyphus brothers' top accountant saw the blip and informed his employers.

The Abido mother pleaded with her youngest child. "Please, Jeffy. Please come home and straighten this out. Charleston doesn't deserve this. They're going to kill him."

"What," pausing to control his breathing, "what did Charlie do, mother?"

"A woman from his work called him to meet at the riverfront docks. She said it was important, but didn't want to discuss it over the phone. Instead, she told him he was connected to millions of missing people. Charlie said there were men wearing ski masks, and they jumped him. He was able to escape, but he's out there, somewhere, hiding. I think it's those Greeks, son."

Staring blankly at a motionless tree, Jefferson's clenched jaw responded, "Give me two weeks, mother."

With Jefferson's charismatic influence and connections, he was able to return to the States with a task force on standby to establish some policies and solutions for the city, including affordable housing and combating illegal gambling and gang violence.

Not even old enough to drink, he defeated the incumbent mayor in a landslide, becoming the city's youngest and first African-American mayor. Many city council members felt the young mayor was over his head, but he won them over when his non-violent, gang truce received the most bipartisan votes in the city's history.

To ensure his city council was in place, the mayor quickly settled matters with the Greek syndicate in an 'off-line' agreement-type accommodation for his brother. The Cyphus brothers agreed to a trade-off, understanding that future concessions would be made. The mayor agreed by way of a handshake.

Splash.

STUMPED

Alana and I stayed outside the top stairs while Sal waited for Cire. I held onto my wife and kissed her under her ear. I wasn't sure if I should confess or just hold her longer for the support of losing my brother. She smelled like she bathed in cinnamon and lemons. She rubbed my back and told me everything would be okay. Puzzled by the recent occurrences, I wasn't sure anything was OK.

"I'm going to help JG even if he's hiding," I told Alana.

Alana studied me. She calculated her thoughts and asked, "Can I ask you something, and don't you lie to me?"

"What's up?"

"Did you think something was going on with JG and me? Don't lie!"

I laughed to buy time and tried not to lie. "Come on, Alana; you've been acting really shady for a while, if I may say so, and you never keep anything from me."

My wife grabbed me by the waist.

"Do you know how hard it was to orchestrate your surprise party, let alone keep Sal quiet about this? I know he'd tell you and then tell you to act surprised."

I tilted my wife's chin toward me and kissed her. "Thank you."

Cire pulled up to the police station in a silver Dodge Minivan. Jevaun was behind him in a white Chrysler Pacifica. Sara was in the front passenger seat.

Though the minivan was the perfect camouflage, his Prada sunglasses vetoed the outfit. "Everything cooked and curry?"

"Let's get somewhere and chop it up."

"I've got the perfect place, Bruv," Cire retorted.

We rode silently before I told him about the interaction in the detective's office. I told him about 'JG' and his findings of incriminating material involving the mayor and other officials. Alana's interactions with her coworker were on the level, and there was no affair, but he was missing.

Cire sucked his teeth, "I knew Alana wouldn't do that to you, Bruv, but I know not to involve myself in married people's business, you know? She part Sistah, part Filipino, Bruv. Those are two of the most loyal creatures Jah makes. You're a silly man, Bruv."

"OK, OK, I get it, C. I get it now, but when all this shit was going on and Sal," I froze.

"Wagwan with Sal, Bruv?"

We slowed to a red light. An older woman picked through a trash can. Before the traffic signal changed, I exited the car and handed the woman a 50-dollar bill. The quick sprint back to the minivan brought on an epiphany. The trash can lady called me a saint from heaven. Cire fist-bumped me and shook his head in approval.

"Sal mentioned Radar would get rid of the person I thought Alana was screwing, but in essence, Alana's coworker was in danger."

"Whatcha saying, Bruv?"

"Sal put Radar on Alana's co-worker."

Cire sucked his teeth.

"I know. Not good."

"Not good at all, Bruv. That dude is meticulous."

I looked at the passing clouds through the minivan's sunroof. One cloud resembled a dog, another a top hat, and a third a rabbit. Did Radar eliminate an innocent man, or did JG vanish before anyone could reach him?

SARYA & GERTIE

We headed out of the city and rode in silence. I appreciated that Cire didn't waste words. Although full of life and comic relief, Sal always had a story to tell. Something to say. Sara and Alana were exhausted with Sal's stories and comments.

We exited off the highway and headed West on a two-lane road. It mimicked a boneyard of old, retired semi-trucks. Old Mack trucks, Peterbilts, Volvos, and Freightliners lined up on each side of the road. Cire knew where we were going, and I left it there, but Sal's text popped up on the minivan's display.

SAL: *Tell me we're not going where I think we are.*

Cire chuckled.

The laugh worried me. "What's up, C?"

"You remember Dirty Gertie and Sarya Brunson, right?"

I searched through the moonroof for more clouds. There were none.

"C, Alana is in the other car, brother," I pleaded. "We can't go wherever we're going."

"You say you want to find the JG character, clear your wife of any suspicion, and nail the mayor, right?"

"Of course, Cire, but consider this," I explained. "We've never involved family in our operations, and this is introducing my wife to the head of the snake—my old snake."

Cire studied me, peeking at the road. "They can help us find Robbie's killer, too, Bruv."

I pinched the bridge of my nose as if that would produce the answer, but could only respond, "Fuck it, man, let's do it. I'll deal with Alana afterward."

"Alana will understand, Bruv, plus that was a long time ago."

Sarya and I embarked on our courtship during our academy days. She was smart enough to gain acceptance to the military leadership program, but her 'around the way' attitude couldn't be broken to respect or show respect to the senior leaders. She washed out of a class and eventually left the program; however, she gained and absorbed enough knowledge to become dangerous in the real world. The military should have placed her off the grid, like Sal. Cire confirmed everything I was thinking.

"What do you think those military brutes do with all that irresistible energy? Sarya was resilient, spunky, and covert, Bruv. They kicked her out of the academy but not out of the system."

My finger traced my face like an esthetician. "I wonder what she's up to?"

"She served in Yemen, Chad, Lebanon, Iraq, and met me and Gertie on a mission in Hungary," Cire stated. "Gertie and I dabbled, but just like us, they do what they do, Bruv. Now we're going to get them to back us up."

"Wow. All these secrets."

Cire snapped his fingers. "Do you remember Frankie Fresh?"

"The drug dealer to the stars, athletes, and the underground?" I asked. "He vanished to London or Ireland or somewhere, right?"

"Pffft! Now that depends on who is telling the story," Cire explained.

"He stole money from Victor Padgette—the head of all European syndicates—and boldly hid from Victor in Victor's own compound for seven months."

"Get the fuck outta here."

"Talk about balls, Bruv," Cire continued. "Frankie got so cocky; he's stealing food from the main house. That's when Gertie and Sarya did their thing. No one has seen him since."

I reflected on my brief yet significant encounter with Sarya from Chester, Pennsylvania. She had a spirited, East Coast swag, complemented by her slim, athletic build, which highlighted her dedication to fitness with toned muscles everywhere. I remember asking her what sports she participated in high school, and she told me, 'All of them.'

It made me more attracted to her graceful stature, like a ballerina. She had an infectious smile, drawing men and women to her. She was magnetic. I always wanted to be near her. Our first date off training grounds resulted in missing the last bus back to campus. She knew she'd be sent home, and I was nervous. I'd never been in trouble yet felt at ease with this captivating ball of energy. Her personality made me trust anything she said or did.

We found a Motel 6, ate a super-sized pepperoni pizza with green and banana peppers, and consumed a six-pack of Hefeweizen. Drawn to Sarya's sparkling eyes and rough laugh, I was mesmerized by how this enchanting person could be so hood yet radiant with sex appeal.

I recall our marathon kissing sessions until my lips became numb. She was confident and experienced, and I was just excited to touch her. We did what normal, horny teens would do and acted out all our sexual fantasies in one evening. I became entangled in new emotions and tension I had never experienced before. She was my first love.

I promised I'd never forget Sarya, but I never dared to reach out to her. With her beauty and brains, I wondered if she became someone's trophy wife or a moment of convenience.

Cire jabbed me on my left shoulder, shoving me to the door panel - all while steering with his left hand.

"Snap out of it, Bruv," he shouted. "You and Sarya are a memory; I'm sure she'll understand this is business. Don't make this shit weird, Bruv."

"True statement," I said. "Let's make it do what it does."

Cire's nostrils flared. We turned off the street onto a gravel pathway. Emerald green Brighter Blooms ushered us a mile to a place where only the initiated would know where to find this dwelling. The architecture resembled someone having stolen a portion of the Louvre Palace. The only thing missing was the Seine River: a blue Mercedes-Benz G-wagon and two black Range Rovers parked face-to-face in the semi-circle driveway.

I whistled.

"Yeah, Bruv, they're doing their thing."

Sal made a beeline for us while Alana and Sara looked in awe at the agave plants and tropical perennials around the miniature chateau. "Dude!"

Cire raised his hand to Sal. "Don't start, Sallie! This is the best strategy for us, plus we need to figure out who took Robbie out."

Sal's shoulders drooped. His sad eyes searched for something to say, but he chose to hug me instead. I patted his back to acknowledge I understood.

"Robbie didn't deserve this, and if Dirty and Sarya can help us, let's do it quickly, but we have to be careful. They know where all the bodies are buried and even more."

I shook my head in agreement, and Alana approached us.

"Um, where are we? Who lives here? And how come you've never brought us here before?" Alana asked.

"Long story, Sweetie, but we're here now, thanks to Cire. You can thank him for this one," I said. "First time for me, too."

Sarya opened the door, and my heart fluttered even in my wife's presence. She greeted us with a big smile and hugged Cire.

"Peace and blessings, dear strangers," Sarya quipped. "Welcome to Casa de la Gorgeous."

The entrance featured a grand staircase with a gray and white checkerboard tile design. "Shit! This place will put Miami's Club Bed to shame," Sal shouted. If it weren't for the LoFi grooves playing over the sound system, Sal's voice would have echoed twice.

Various-sized beds and mattresses were scattered throughout the open room. Hot pink pillows provided a distinct accent to the fire-engine red couches and beds. Multiple couches that resembled lips laced the walls, and patchouli invaded my nostrils.

Alana's eyes explored the venue and poked me in the ribs. "Where are we?"

I shrugged and told her, "This is one of C's points of contact who's going to help us find JG and maybe locate the people who killed Robbie."

That settled my wife's inkling, but her antennas were up. She told Sara to stay close as Sarya escorted us to another room. I did my best to ignore Sarya's athletic frame. Then I spotted a voluptuous Dirty Gertie in a fluorescent red, shoe-shaped lounge chair, pulling on her marijuana-filled cigar.

She searched the smoke as it evaporated in the air before she surprised us with her nine-millimeter.

"What are you madaphuqs doing in my place?

CONFLICTION

Dirty Gertie pointed her piece at us with one hand and maintained her blunt with the other. We froze with our hands up, not knowing if she was earnest. She peered through us, attempting to discern our basis for being in her place. She studied me as if I were a family member. Her eyes burned a hole in my forehead, and the weed's aroma grew stronger. I was sure I was getting high while terrified by the standoff. No one moved or said anything. Sara hid behind me, and I swallowed hard. I would say something to break the tension, but Gertie spoke first.

"I only agreed to let you madaphuqs here because I owe that sexy, chocolate man a huge favor," Gertie said, pointing her pistol briefly at Cire. "This place is, hmm, what's another word for anonymous, pretty gyal?"

Sara peeked from behind me. "Me?"

"Yes, you!" Gertie snapped. "You're the only pretty gyal in here, cept me and Sarya. What's another word?"

Sara thought for a moment and responded, "Um, Nameless? Unidentifiable? Unknown? Discreet?"

Gertie snapped her French-manicured fingers. "Right! All that—especially discreet. This place is discreet, and we don't need any additional heat, but I think we're in the same boat with some constituents of the young Mayor."

Sarya approached Gertie and snatched the gun. "You're scaring the girl and her momma, Gert. Stop with the bullshit. Y'all can put your hands down. She knew y'all were coming."

"Whew, Gertie," Sal exhaled. "You scared the hell outta me with your eyebrows looking like the Dark Knight. No offense. Can I get a hug, a drink, or something to eat? Hell, I might need to take a shit."

Sal left the area, and Gertie took another pull on her blunt and shifted towards me.

"Is he always like this?"

"Lots to unpack with Sal. Blame his parents for naming him Salvatore, but you know the deal. How've you been, Gertie?"

She closed her eyes and yawned, stretching her henna-designed arms and hands. Eleven or more bracelets and bangles slid down to her forearms. Her braless breasts filled her floral kimono, and though Alana was standing next to me, I couldn't look away from her number two pencil eraser-shaped nipples piercing the material. Her navel ring teased all of us.

"Hi, I'm Alana, Chuck's wife. This pretty 'gyal' you called upon is our daughter, Sara. I understand you and your colleague can help us with a few things, and we're very appreciative."

Gertie looked past Alana and rolled her eyes.

Sarya faced my wife and extended her hand. "Gertie's bark is worse than her bite. She gets bored when we're not open for business."

My wife asked, "What kind of establishment is this place?"

Sarya responded, looking at me, "We like to call this establishment a place where people can escape reality. It's a lifestyle."

Sal returned with a sniffer of brown liquor and chirped, "It's a sex club."

"C'mon, Bruv," Cire chimed in. "This ain't what it looks like, Alana."

"I'm not judging," Alana responded. "However, if you don't mind my asking, I'm curious how this helps us."

Sarya and Gertie looked at each other with the 'you tell them' challenge. With her index finger and thumb, Gertie took another pull from the shrinking blunt.

"It's normal behavior," she said, exhaling smoke. "It's what people do. It's how that pretty gyal of yours got here, right? All we do is create a refuge to romp, a haven for sensuality, and a sanctuary to swing. People come here to satisfy their desires without the fear of retribution. To us, it's a place of business and our cover. We reap significant benefits and work covert operations in plain sight, but off the beaten path. No one remembers our faces because they're too busy protecting their own."

Alana studied Gertie. More questions swirled. "So, how did you get involved in this industry?"

"Pfft! This isn't an industry," the woman responded. "What's the population of India? Do you know without asking Google? I'll tell you. Over a billion people. A billion and a half. Do you know how they got to a billion and a half? By fucking."

Sal laughed, spitting out some of his drink, "Seriously?"

"Yes, Sal," Sarya interrupted. "People are fucking all the time. Sorry, pretty gyal. About 140 million people worldwide are fucking right now, so this isn't an industry. It's a normal business place that's a secret, although we all do it."

Alana adjusted her Warby Parker frames, the faint gleam of the lenses catching the light as she squinted, taking in every corner of the room she'd once admired. She cleared her throat and asked, "Again, with all due respect to your beautiful and elaborate place, what does this have to do with my husband's brother and my missing co-worker?"

Dirty Gertie shifted in her seat and extended her spine, causing her nipples to catch my attention again. A collection of specially wrapped cigar leaves sat on a glass table, with four black, porcelain booties serving as its base. She lit another spliff and took a long pull, causing her to cough like a chain smoker. Sal ran over to pat her back, but Gertie waved him off.

"Magnus Kwafu. Heard of him?"

No one responded, so Gertie continued.

"He was an uncanny patron here. I can spot the problems when they walk in the door, but he could only get here through membership, invitation, or with a woman." Gertie stated.

"This Magnus character applies for a membership and pays cash up front. Not a red flag, per se, because most people don't use their credit cards. "

"We're discreet, though," Sarya interrupted. "If someone uses their credit card, it displays CHARITY."

Gertie sucked her teeth and continued, "Considering his role at the university, we assumed he would be discreet and honor our rules.

"He was the university's director of financial aid, ya know. This rassclot was embezzling money from the uni and admitting students to college under the table for $5,000 cash. For each."

Gertie took another hit. I lost count of how many blunts she smoked since we arrived.

"This bumbaclot starts showing up regularly on costume nights and buying up the bar during beginner nights. Those are new member nights. Then, he starts partying with the swinger crowd, hooking up with one particular couple, and meeting regularly. You know how it goes when people get turned out. His lack of discretion and frivolous spending give him diarrhea of the mouth."

Cire sucked his teeth. "What an idiot."

Sarya said, "What's worse is that he brought attention to our establishment. Now that he's a card-carrying member, he can bring guests with him, and this moron brings a fucking undercover reporter here. This chick ends up writing an exposé on Magnus and our place."

"Damn!" Sal shouted. He was finishing his second or third drink.

"Magnus gets investigated, fired, and then arrested. We canceled his membership, and he believes we are somehow connected to his arrest, based on the article. He shows up demanding to have his membership restored. Security prevents him, and he starts vandalizing the vehicles of our patrons.

"Bad move," Cire said, shaking his head.

"Good and bad," Gertie stated between more puffs. "We attracted patrons from all walks of life, including politicians and other officials. Some showed up to check things out. Look around and do business. Others realized how discreet our place was in helping them get their rocks off. Sarya and I kept tabs to see if any of these people were scum buckets, Magnus being one of them."

Alana raised her hand like a polite schoolgirl. "Robbie? My co-worker? The mayor?"

"I'm getting to that," Gertie snapped. "Like I said, mahdaphuqs came in here looking to screw but be discreet. They spent a lot of money on their high-end cars, flaunting their power, and getting their work done."

"A local high school principal gained momentum right before the Mayor won his seat. The buzz was that people were backing this school guy. He had a lot of mahaphuqs in his corner, ya know? One night, he shows up with this guy who owns all the Burger Kings around here. What's his name, Sarya?"

Sarya searched the ceiling for the name. "I don't know, Gert; he's known as the BK Prince."

"Yeah, yeah. The BK Prince!" Gertie clapped. "He comes in here with him, but the BK guy left all pissed and shit because the principal brought some barely twenty-year-old cheerleaders to screw."

Alana was losing her patience with Dirty Gertie, but Gert was someone you did not rush.

"Next time we see the BK Prince, he's in here with the mayor backing his campaign and the principal - get this shit - is indicted by a federal grand jury for his participation in a large-scale drug trafficking organization."

Alana turned to me and Sal. "Do you think all of this is connected?"

"That's why we're here, Dear." I replied, "to get the answers and some help."

Sarya chimed in, "Y'all mustn't watch the news and shit. The principal hanged himself, claiming his innocence in a letter and pointing the finger at the mayor's brother for shady doings, which was his platform from the beginning.

"After the principal died, the mayor and his top dogs, including the BK Prince, showed up regularly. Not that it's any of our business, but we have cams and mics all over the place, and I'm sure one of the Cyphus brothers' lieutenants was at the table."

Cire looked as if he had seen Lazarus rise from the dead. "The Cyphus brothers?"

"Yes, C," Sarya acknowledged.

Sara approached us, displaying a news article on her cell phone. It described the principal's indictment charges with possession and conspiring to distribute fentanyl, cocaine, heroin, and oxycodone. Two former high school cheerleaders testified and helped Metro identify the principal.

The cheerleaders were arrested following a routine traffic stop when the police found fentanyl and heroin in the trunk. They claimed innocence and informed the police that the principal forced them to deliver drugs.

"This guy is wicked," Alana said. "This has to be some of the stuff on that laptop JG had with names, numbers, and affiliates. I don't blame him for disappearing."

Reading the article on the phone, Cire shook his head. "This mayor has dirty and bad people protecting him."

Cire paced the area, waiting for the answer to hit him. "This is a different kind of party if the Cyphus brothers are involved, and one thing is certain, Bruv, the Mayor is dirty."

Lurching, Sal stumbled into the conversation.

"Who knew the mayor had a brova? Anybody?"

Cire sucked his teeth and stomped his foot - embarrassed at Sal's drunken behavior.

"Gimme dat glass, Sal," Cire mumbled, grabbing Sal's arm. "You've been acting like a fool's ass since we got here. What's wrong with you, Bruv?"

Sal shrugged his shoulders.

"Get it together!" Sal bowed.

Sarya led us to another part of the chateau where her chef prepared some of Alana's favorite Filipino cuisine. How did she know? However they played it, the chef brought his A-game with slow-cooked Adobo soaked in the right vinegar, soy sauce, garlic, pepper, served with brown rice and beef marrow stew. Alana was in heaven.

"Who in the hell flew in from the islands to cook this?" Alana celebrated. "This is fabulous!"

"We aim to please in all facets, Momma," Gertie explained. "We're gonna spend some time together, so why not enjoy the company with a happy belly?"

Sara chimed in, "What about my swim meet next week, Daddy? Can Gertie escort me to the meet and, you know, protect me?"

My heart sank, "Why do you think you would need protecting, sweetie?"

"Uh, Uncle Robbie?"

Damn. Everything was moving so fast; I didn't realize that someone was out there looking to take me out for something I likely did or didn't do. The thought of the past catching up to me and my family with a target on their backs made my neck throb.

I needed to plan a burial for my brother, keep my family safe, and find JG. And it surprised me, Sara gravitated to Dirty Gertie so fast. It was clearly a sign.

Gertie didn't need an excuse to pull out her nine, but she raised it in the air. "We've got people like you have people, Chuck, so if Sara needs extra eyes at her meet, we've got her. Go put your brother to rest."

"I appreciate this, Gertie," I conveyed. "I think we should return to our normal routines. It's the only way we'll find out who's behind all this madness."

Sarya sashayed over to me and tapped my shoulder. Stoic and serious, the casual, social encounter was over. Her gaze presented a "I know something" look.

"I need to holla at you in private. Another day and time, though. After, you know, Sara and Robbie."

"Cool," pretending like her death stare didn't bother me. "Do you want to chop it up outside real quick?"

Sarya shook her head. "After you settle your affairs for your brother. It can wait, but not too much longer, bet?"

I nodded in agreement but hesitated to retort.

ANTICIPATION

School flags, banners, and face-painted students were everywhere—posted signs displaying their favorite swimmer's name and fat heads of athletes. Surprisingly, the PA system blasted a Talib Kweli song, and most adults appreciated the music. Coaches huddled with their athletes, providing encouragement and last-minute instructions. Other people around the starting blocks appeared to be judges or other officials, checking the timing systems to record the results.

As promised, Gertie posted up closest to Sara and her swim mates. She did her best to blend in with the rest of the parents, students, and onlookers, wearing Sara's school colors. Cloaked in a blueish hoodie, matching sweatpants, and orange and yellow Nike Interact running shoes, Gertie passed as a mom, coach, or someone's auntie. Somewhere within that fitted frame and garments was a full arsenal of weaponry.

I saw my daughter wearing her pink Beats by Dre headphones, focused and stretching with one of her teammates. Sara's intense pre-game drill, before each swim meet, combined ballistic stretching and yoga to push her muscles beyond their normal range of motion. It was not a regime made for anyone with a weak stomach. I wondered what she was listening to. Her hype song was Mobb Deep's *Shook Ones*. A proud moment to know she embraced her dad's Boom Bap playlist.

I sat diagonally from Gertie with my eyes on the pool's entrance. There were multiple entrances to the natatorium, but only one way for admittance.

Cire sat in a sling chair in the opposite corner, wearing a University of Maryland - Eastern Shore Swimming hoodie, a matching hat, gray Fabletics joggers, and all white Nike Pegasus runners. He fit the scout part with a clipboard and a stopwatch. He undoubtedly possessed a Smith & Wesson 380 in a shoulder holster and a Springfield Hellcat by his ankle.

I scanned the area as the dazzling lights beamed down on the pool. I wanted to see if anyone else seemed out of place or out of character. Alana and another mother sat in the center of the bleachers. Sarya was three rows above them. I imagined others were flanking throughout the area for protection. I did not know anyone from Gertie's crew other than Sarya.

The air was thick with anticipation. If I were a candy, I would be a bag of chocolate, filled with excitement and nerves. Sara pre-qualified past the preliminary heats due to her times and waited for the final.

This was it - the 400-meter freestyle championship against her school rival, Daisy Riley, the reigning queen of the pool. Sara finished third to Daisy in an earlier meet and second in last year's state championship.

More people filled the bleachers, everyone lit with eagerness and already hyped. Alana pulled out a bright sign decorated with glitter and colorful letters: *"GO SARA."*

Daisy removed her warmups near the starting blocks. She saw Alana's sign and chuckled with a smug, trademark smile plastered across her face.

She taunted the crowd, threatening to boo her. "Get ready for a show!" Daisy flexed her muscles as if she were on a pose-down stage. A few cheers but more boos ensued as the reigning champion adjusted her goggles.

I saw Sara swallow her nervousness, and the determination to win returned. She was not going to allow Daisy's antics to cloud her space. As the starting whistle blew, it felt as though time had slowed down. Sara and the rest of the competitors gripped the starting blocks, waiting for the gun to fire.

"Set? POW!"

Sara dove into the water, and the world above her faded away, replaced by the rhythmic sound of water surging around her. Her strokes were powerful and fluid. With each turn, Sara could hear the cheers from the stands. I clapped rhythmically with each stroke and yelled, "Do it for Uncle Robbie!" Why did I say that?

I could hear Alana shouting, "Focus, Sara," as I imagined my daughter had visions of her uncle, who always believed in her, flashing in her mind, wishing he were there to cheer her on.

Approaching the final lap, Sara caught a glimpse of Daisy, who was slightly ahead. She moved like a pro; a kid with a bright future, but I could see my daughter surge with every kick. She couldn't let her rival win, not today.

With everything she had, she pushed as the crowd yelled, screamed, and cheered for the competitors.

"Push, Sara, push," I rang out. "You've got this, girl! Come on, girl; push!"

In the final stretch, Sara summoned every ounce of strength, legs snapping into one last furious kick. She surged ahead and slammed into the wall first, chest heaving. For a beat, the pool was silent — then the buzzer blared, and the scoreboard lit up. Sara's lane flashed. A new state and national record. She hadn't just beaten Daisy. She'd dethroned her. Sara was the new queen of the pool.

Alana's composure cracked, joy spilling down her cheeks as she sprinted to her daughter. Sara wrapped her arms tight around her mother, the crowd exploding in cheers as teammates swarmed them.

"You did it!"

I fought my way through the frenzy and kissed my daughter on the crown of her wet head.

"You were incredible, girlie!"

"Uncle Robbie was in that pool with me, Dad," she whispered, eyes wide with conviction. "I swear I could hear him telling me 'Give it all you got, sweetie.'"

The words lodged in my throat. Knowing I wouldn't see Robbie again, the weight of her words made it hard to swallow. I shut my eyes, and the tears burned past my lashes.

"He was here, baby," I murmured, draping a towel around her shoulders. "He was here, and he always will be."

The emotions suddenly shifted. I was hit with a moment of déjà vu, as I felt the same eerie feeling that had prickled at my birthday party. In my peripheral vision, I sensed the Colombian was to my right. Watching. Paranoia overcame me.

My pulse spiked. I searched the area for my team. Where was Cire? His sling chair was empty. Gertie was nowhere to be found. I scanned the area for Sarya, but there was too much commotion around Sara.

I slipped away from the high schoolers as my phone buzzed. Cire's text glared up at me:

WE GOT COMPANY.

The world detonated. Mayhem ensued as three sharp cracks ripped the air. Children scrambled, some plunging into the pool in blind panic, others ducking under bleachers, bodies colliding as chaos swept the arena. Security was useless — outnumbered and overwhelmed. A tournament official shouted for calm, his voice drowned by terror.

I spun back for Alana and Sara, but Gertie already had them by the shoulders, shoving them toward the locker rooms.

A piercing *zing* sliced past my ear, hot and close, like a wasp grazing flesh. I froze, lungs clamped, adrenaline detonating in my veins. Instinct pulled me down, rolling to the side as another round cracked overhead.

Then—a scream. High-pitched. Horrific. It cut through the madness, echoing across the arena.

"No! Oh my god, oh my god, someone help us," a woman yelled. Her husband crumpled over, clutched his shoulder, and screeched in pain. His shirt rapidly stained crimson as panic continued to erupt around me.

"Someone call 911!" screamed a kid nearby. Medical trainers who commonly treat athletic injuries rushed to the suffering man's side. Trembling in fear and disbelief of violence, the medical staff aided the wounded man.

I caught my breath as reality struck. I was in a daze, realizing those parents weren't the target. A sharp, commanding, and recognizable voice got my attention, yanking my arm and pulling me to safety.

"Yo, we gotta go." Sarya's urgent tone was imposing and direct. "Stay low and keep moving!"

"Where's Sara and Alana?"

"Gert's got 'em."

I could still hear the man groaning in agony. A commotion ensued around us, with panicked cries, as the wails of police and emergency sirens approached in the distance.

Two more gunshots rang out. Then a third. We instinctively ducked lower. More screams blurred. Hysteria flowed through me, and I turned toward the pool. Sarya gripped my arm. "Gert's got them. Move out!"

DISARRAY

I sent a cryptic message to the team to meet at the safe house. Cire confirmed. Sara and Alana were safe with Gertie.

We drove in silence. The engine hum was the loudest thing between Sarya and me. Despite what happened at the pool, the highway appeared empty. I was lost in thoughts, still feeling the whizzing by my ear. I checked for blood a few times, but to no avail.

Sarya gripped the steering wheel as if she were holding it in place. She pierced through the windshield, driving intently beyond the speed limit. She glanced at me, her lips parting as if to say something, and she hesitated. She wanted to tell me something, but was reluctant. That wasn't like Sarya. A few minutes ago, she alluded to bullets, which would get me to safety. Now, she sped through the streets with her jaws clenched.

"We need to talk." Sarya broke the silence.

"What is it, Sarya?"

Taking a deep breath, Sarya retorted, "What are you thinking? Like, seriously, dude, what are you thinking?"

"Right now, or in general, because a lot of shit is going on in my mind, ya know?"

"Aside from you almost getting a crescent blown into your head, you put everyone in jeopardy, Chuck."

"I know, I…"

"I'm not finished," Sarya interrupted. "If this madman really wanted you clipped, he would have done it. Splash, end of story.

That was truly a warning shot to let you know he was close and you were exposed."

Sarya was right, and before I admitted it, she continued, "You're not thinking straight, dude, and I hate to break it to you, but something's shady with your guy, too."

"Who?"

"Sally."

"What did you just say to me?"

Sarya looked in the rearview for a beat, over to me, and back to the road, and shook her head.

"What's on your mind, Sarya?"

"Where's Sal, Chuck? Where's your homie and his BFF, Radar? Were they at the pool to protect your daughter? To protect you? Do they even know how serious this is? Where are they, Chuck? It's been two weeks since we met at the club. Your family is in danger, somebody's firing at will and terrorizing high school kids, and where is your confidant? Is he tracking the Colombian or the Mayor and the friggin Cyphus brothers? They are the epitome of deadbeat! Have you called him or, better yet, when's the last time he's called you?"

I pulled my phone from my pocket. The bottom part of the screen was cracked due to the chaos at the pool, but it appeared to be functional. My thumbprint opened the device. No messages. No missed calls.

To defend the situation, I said, "Sal's always been incog, and the stories about Radar are true. His cover is undercover, you know?"

Sarya took a deep breath, brushed her hair to the side with her hand, and shook her head.

"I don't know how to say this, so I'm just going to say it. I'm not feeling or trusting anyone on your team except Cire and Jevaun. Everyone else? Sketchy, and I'm speaking from field experience, Chuck, and my intuition. Something's off."

The rest of the ride was in silence. Sarya touched a nerve, and the tension filled the car like fog. I was overwhelmed with fear, anger, and now a sense of curiosity. Where the fuck was Sal? And Radar? Surely, I would have received a text or something from either of them, letting me know they were around to protect Sara. Sarya was right.

My phone buzzed—a text from an unknown number.

Almost puto. Almost.

My neck and ears burned with anger. I showed Sarya the text. She shook her head and mumbled something.

"This guy is fucking with you, Chuck."

I stared out the window, watching night arrive. I crossed my arms, but that brought no comfort to the tension in my chest. I massaged the bridge of my nose, then my temples, as the sun was taking its place beyond the horizon.

DOUBT

Back at the safehouse, the dim glow of the streetlights flickered through the windows. Cire paced in one direction, and I was back and forth opposite him. My mind raced.

"Y'all look like two emcees on stage right about now," Sarya quipped. "Both of y'all sit down so we can figure this out."

"I saw him," Cire said. "I saw dat wahala, Bruv. It was the same guy who, you know, got Robbie. He was at the pool."

I showed them the random text message.

Gertie had her nine-millimeter at her side. "Fuck!"

"We're being reactive right now, and it's time to get proactive. You," Gertie pointed to me. "Let's go to your house. I need to see your place. Sarya, you and Jevaun are staying. Cire's with us."

"Yo, Jevaun, have you heard from Sallie?" I asked my dreadlocked friend.

"C'mon, Chuck, I would've put you on game a long time ago if I knew something," Jevaun responded. "Sal, be on some bullshit at times. That's why I fucks with you as point guard."

"He's always been a lightning rod," I stated. "But even this feels different considering the circumstances."

Sarya walked by the window, peering out into the parking lot and darkened streets. The light from the movie theater teased and tinted the evening clouds. My eyes lingered on Sarya's body longer than I should have. I questioned how long my gaze at Sarya's rump was right in front of Alana. My heart raced as I wondered if Alana was looking at me, looking at Sarya. Sarya turned from the window and said, "I pray I'm wrong about Sal; for your sake, Chuck."

That broke my trance. "Me?"

Sarya glared, "I'm the nice one. Gertie doesn't play fair, and she won't give two shits that Sal is your friend. I know her, Chuck. She's on one. When women and children are involved, it's the next level for her."

Sarya's eyes brightened wide with seriousness. She wasn't the person I fell in love with many moons ago, but her eyes were still the same, and she told a different story. I heeded the sign and hugged my daughter before I left. I told Cire I was ready to bounce and kissed Alana. She waved her phone to let me know whether to call or text once I was good. I understood the hint and winked.

Cire zoomed us through the city in a Cadillac CT5 Sport. Gertie sat on the passenger side, popping her cinnamon-flavored gum with every third chew. The constant popping was incredibly irritating, and I couldn't wait to get out of the car.

"Did you know, in the ancient days of Greece and Rome, criminals and slaves were marked with tattoos," Gertie asked.

Neither Cire nor I responded. We knew Gertie would continue.

"Madaphuqs tattooed the bad boys and girlies so everyone would see their markings like the scarlet letter. Egyptians tattoo themselves as a form of protection. Asians marked themselves from a cultural perspective."

Cire sucked his teeth.

Curiosity stomped me. "Where are you going with this, Gertie?"

"I'm thinking out loud, mind-mapping, and wishing I had a blunt or some dark liquor. Do you have any Hennessy at your house?"

"There's probably some Crown in there, and I definitely have Uncle Nearest. Both 1856 and 1884."

"Lovely, that will work for me," Gertie applauded. "Another historical memory that will manifest. I wonder how many madaphuqs stole our inventions and became famous off our labor?"

"Countless," Cire chimed in. "Chuck, text your nosy-ass neighbor and tell him we need his garage, a'ight, Bruv?"

"On it."

Phil responded in seconds. Gertie pulled a micro weapon from her sleeve.

"What's that?"

Cire laughed. "Dirty has all kinds of heat, Bruv."

Gertie held it between the bucket seats for a better view. "It's a three-in-one. This blade can do more damage than any bullet when used properly, and this part is the million-volt stun gun that can drop the biggest of the bigs."

"And what's number three?"

"Oh," Gertie remembered. "Flashlight with multiple settings, mainly used to blind or disorient someone with its brightness."

"I need one of those, Gert, maybe a couple for my girls."

Gertie laughed. "Sara has one."

"Yo, Bruv, peep!"

Cire pointed to a pile of sunflower seed shells near my curb. There was only one person who'd do that.

"Dat mudaphuq Sallie was here," Gertie barked.

I ventured to disagree, as this could have been a setup. Sal could have been watching my house, or someone placed them there to lead us down a mistaken path. I asked my nosy neighbor.

"Hard to say, Chuck, Pierre had a massive cookout for his granddaughter's birthday. Cars were lined up on both sides of the street. I didn't see anything unusual after that. We can check my security monitor if you like."

"Gimme dem keys," Gertie ordered. "We don't have time to deliberate on whether date madaphuq was here or if he's in the house. If he's in the house, he gets dealt with. We got work to do."

Gertie approached my home, displaying her extensive discipline as she swept the house. She held her Dan Wesson Dex pistol with a 19-round magazine close to her and ready. Cire followed, signaling a number one sign for me to wait a beat while they cleared the first floor. He was carrying a Smith & Wesson 357 Magnum with a silencer. I had my old faithful Glock by my side.

Gertie entered the house and moved from my living room to the kitchen, office, and guest bedrooms. She maneuvered tightly and closed around the corners to alleviate danger or blind spots. It was as if she had pre-planned her systematic moves through the first floor. Cire swept the dining area, sitting room, and game room before he reappeared, giving me the peace sign to head upstairs.

Gertie took up the rear, still monitoring movement from the first floor. After we cleared the house, we sat on the couch to view the footage of Robbie's attack. Gertie sat between Cire and me, studying the footage. I also showed her hacked footage from the neighbors' homes. At the sight of the Colombian, she leaped to her feet, pointing at the screen.

"Rhatid!"

"What is it, Gertie?"

"Dat mahdaphuq is El Cucuy!"

Cire rested his hands on his bald head. "Shiiiiiiit! This ain't good, Bruv."

"What? Who is he? Who the fuck is this guy? What does Cucuy mean?"

Gertie stomped around the room like a toddler having a tantrum. She spoke something in Patois while she circled the island in my kitchen. Calming her breathing, she shuffled back to the TV. She viewed the screen again and flailed her arms at me. I wrapped my arms around her to prevent being hit. Gertie grabbed my face with her hands, scratching my ears with her French-manicured nails.

With a tremble in her voice, Gertie said, "Chuck, get that bottle of 1856 and pour several ounces for all of us. That man, that Colombian, that mahdaphuq is El Cucuy, the boogieman."

"Wha-What?"

"You thought Radar was a badass," Gertie pierced. "He is the sensei. You and your crew must have seriously pissed off someone. Like the stories people used to tell their kids, El Cucuy lives in the mountains or caves of Suriname or wherever he comes from. Whatever the case, that mahdaphuq is in your city, and he won't stop with your Robbie - God bless his soul. He will take out everyone in the crew. I need to make a phone call. I'll be back."

My insides twisted and hardened. I lowered to sit down, which felt like minutes to perch.

Cire massaged his chin, babbling something I couldn't understand.

FEVERISH

Dirty Gertie returned to the room with more bounce to her body. In the fifteen minutes she was away, her eyes appeared red from tears or an interrupted nap.

"Si mi ya! Bring the drinks outside. I need to smoke."

"Tell us what's on your mind," Cire stroked Gertie's arm.

"You keep doing that, and other things will be on my mind. We need to focus, C." Gertie sat next to me. "I have a plan, Chuck; you might not like this, but El Cucuy is not your typical mercenary killer. He's devious, crafty, treacherous, and a savage mahdaphuq."

I felt jittery as I suspected what was next. "He's coming back."

Gertie nodded. "But that's a good thing because we know he's going to make a move."

"Like Sara's swim meet," Cire snapped.

"Right, but that was just a warning to let us know he was close."

"Damn, Sarya said the same thing," I remembered. I swallowed air and asked, "What's the deal? What do we do?"

My heart pounded. Before we created any plan and figured out what to do with the Boogieman, I wanted to ensure Alana and Sara were safe.

Gertie set the plan in motion.

"After we do what we do, you, your wife, and daughter will take a long trip, but we gotta make sure this goes as planned."

I nodded.

Gertie placed a sheet of paper on the patio table. She lit her blunt and took a few short puffs. The next puff was deliberate, and she held it for a beat before gently exhaling. She offered Cire and me, but we preferred sipping our whiskey instead.

Gertie made some markings. "It's time to say goodbye to Robbie, Chuck. We'll have a real funeral service right here. Cire is your guy long-range and will clip that mahdaphuq the moment he makes a move. I sent for my ladies to decoy as relatives. They'll be ready to light his ass up, too."

Cire patted my shoulder. "I already like the way this plan is going down, Bruv."

"This cemetery is on the outskirts of town," Cire continued. "It's isolated with plenty of places to hide. We'll see him coming and bomboclaat his ass!"

I went into a deep trance, thinking about how my brother was killed. I'm going to face this boogieman. We laid out the plans as the night air became still. The cadence of crickets set the tone, and stars appeared a little brighter.

I walked by the pool and turned the lights on. I studied the movement of the water, thinking about Sara's swim meet. She told us Robbie was there in the water with her. My heart flickered. I took several deep breaths to compose my nerves. "Wooo-saaaa."

"You alright, Bruv?" Cire's voice broke through my trance. His brows furrowed with concern.

I forced a smile. All this shit was becoming unbearable. Before I could respond, my phone pinged. I figured it was Alana checking on me, but it was quite a surprise.

Hey Bro-ski. U around? We need to talk.

Sal!

The text sent a jolt of anger and unreadiness through my body. Something seemed off with Sal for the past few weeks, and now, the text message came while we were conveniently at the house. I held the phone up so Cire could read the message. He sucked his teeth. "Bumbaclot.'

I paced my pool, thinking of a response. Was Sal nearby, watching us? Why so cryptic? I punched in a response, deleted it, and typed another.

I'm a lil busy. Can it wait?

I hit send. Cire and I walked back to the patio table. I showed Gertie the text.

"What in the actual hell?"

"I know," I chimed. "I'm starting to believe Sarya's suspicions of Sallie. This has been my friend for as long as I've been alive."

Cire walked around the table and studied Gertie's drawing of the cemetery. He took another swig of whiskey. "People change, Bruv."

Gertie laughed. "Well, that's philosophical. Chuck, Sal knows you. He knows how you think, how you move, how you operate."

"If this mahdaphuq is in cahoots with El Cucuy, we've got problems. One thing working for us is he doesn't know shit about our plans."

Forcing another smile, I called Alana. I wanted to ensure she and Sara were safe. She picked up on the first ring. She told me she and Sarya were chatting while Jevaun and Sara were watching a movie. I wondered what that chat consisted of, but both women were as discreet as great chess or poker players, never revealing too much until.

"Lemme speak to Jevaun."

"What it do?"

I gave Jevaun a rundown of Gertie, recognizing the Colombian. I told him about the plan to take out El Cucuy and Sal's text. Jevaun suggested moving to another safehouse to protect Alana and Sara. I didn't think it was a bad idea; however, Sal knew all our hiding spots, plus I didn't want to frighten Sara.

Thoughts raced through my mind of Sal betraying me, betraying my family, betraying the crew. Anger clawed at me, and the fear of something happening to my family shook me.

"Look, ain't shit happening with me and Sarya on point," Jevaun stated with sheer Philly confidence. "Whether we stay or go somewhere else, we good, ya heard? Any signs of trouble, it's going down, but nothing's happening to your family."

Another text appeared. *Wing spot. Tomorrow.*

Gertie and Cire examined Sal's text and conversed as if I wasn't there.

"We can't worry about Sal right now; we've got bigger fish to fry with Cucuy," Gertie stated.

"Yeah, but Sal might be a connection to all of this, G. We gotta think this through before we work this other stuff out."

Gertie slammed the table.

"No! We forge ahead and ice this El Cucuy mahdaphuq first. Trussme, he is calculated and will strike like a cobra again and again until we're dropped. If Sallie's involved, he'll show his face." Gertie pointed at me. "No wing spot, Chuck. We got shit to work out."

UNANTICIPATED

Dr. Goyle leaned against his office door. He was conversing with his physician's assistant about the recent advances in AI and biometric data analysis that potentially support and hinder patients. He also presented her with a $250 American Express gift card for her work anniversary. He knew he wasn't the easiest to work with or work for, but he wanted to keep Ava Howard around.

Not only was she a positive PA who actively listened to the patients and had a thorough understanding of treatment options, but she was also a key component of Dr. Goyle's patient care team. It didn't help that she reminded him of Meagan Good.

Ava shook Dr. Goyle's hand and expressed her appreciation with a church-side hug. He wondered if he should have made the gift card for an even $300 or more, but brushed it off. He gave Ava and the staff the rest of the day off. He wanted to work on a new serum.

He sauntered to his laboratory, where the Afternoon Jazz radio station on Spotify overshadowed the hum of the fluorescent lights. Dr. Goyle put on his nitrile gloves for chemical resistance and prepared to work.

He recalled Cire telling him his latest creation worked like a charm on the African niece, and he wanted to perfect it more.

The doctor wanted the next concoction to be precise and powerful; his masterpiece. He added an extra drop of propofol and used his other supply of midazolam and etomidate to intensify the serum. This would sedate an adult elephant, and he took pride in its effectiveness.

Dr. Goyle was bopping along to the jazzy vibes when a knock at the door startled him. He just released everyone over thirty minutes ago, so he wasn't expecting anyone. He took off his gloves, unbuttoned his lab coat, and opened the door.

The hallway smelled faintly of Mint Listerine, which made the doctor sneeze. He walked down the hallway near the reception desk, and there were no signs of anyone. Lights off and computers in sleep mode. As the doctor made his way back to the lab, he saw an unlabeled package at the door. He puckered his lips out of curiosity. He walked down the opposite hallway, looking for somebody who could have left the package, but the path was dark. Motion sensors would have triggered the lights to stay on.

Dr. Goyle tucked the box under his arm and returned to the lab. He locked the door behind him and returned to a new sedative. He placed new gloves on and turned to the box. He grabbed a medical blade and made a long, precise incision to open the box. A purple Crown Royal bag lay flat in clear bubble wrap, making the doctor laugh aloud.

He pulled a glass vial from the velvet bag. He studied the liquid, shaking the vial to see if any other substances would appear, but to no avail, so he uncorked the vial to inspect the scent.

Dr. Goyle's eyes bulged, and his chest seized. He felt a burning sensation in his lungs and a sharp pinch to his heart as he staggered back, waving his arms to brace his fall. The vial shattered on the floor as the doctor gasped for air. His lungs refused to obey. Stumbling back on his feet, he knocked over equipment, desperately attempting to reach the oxygen mask.

He pulled his cell phone from his pocket and hit Ava's name. He tried to cough, but the air reversed, bringing waste and soiling his pants. Still reaching for the oxygen mask, his vision blurred. Black and green dots danced in front of him and sent him crashing face-first to the floor. The sensation of millions of fire ants attacking him traumatized him. He trembled and choked, kicking the box on its side.

A note with scribbled writing fell out.

For Diatta, you puta! - El Cucuy

PANDEMONIUM

It was time to say goodbye to Robbie — whether I wanted to or not.

My little brother. The one who wouldn't hurt an ant, no matter how much it bit him.

I remembered the three of us as kids — Robbie, Corey Bronson, and me — running from Joshua Hampton, the neighborhood bully. Josh was Milky Way chocolate in complexion, with stormy gray eyes that looked like trouble even before he spoke. His hair was a wild fro, full of lint that had clearly taken up permanent residence — rent-free — from whatever blanket or pillow he'd last slept on.

And that smile. Crooked. Mean—a warning. Get too close, and you'd catch the sour reek of his breath before you caught his fist.

Everyone in our group agreed Josh should have been in a reform school for boys for his antics at school and in the streets, but he certainly didn't belong around us.

Corey lived two houses from Robbie and me and walked - mostly ran - with us after the school bus let us off at the corner. The minute he jumped from the school bus steps, he'd cram between us, nervous and fearful of Josh. On an overcast day, we began our trek to our houses to avoid getting soaked by the rain.

Corey was close to tears as Josh followed us and called us names. I remember pointing to his house and telling him we were close when Robbie turned to us and flashed the OK sign. He did a military face and charged Josh. I attempted to grab his jacket, but he pulled away from me.

"What are you doing, Robbie? Are you crazy?"

Robbie screeched like an eagle and lunged at our neighborhood enemy, flailing fists of fury, frustration, and fear, punching Josh's cheeks and nose until blood spewed from his nostrils.

Our adversary curled into the fetal position, protecting his face from Robbie's repeated knocks on his head as if they were a door. Corey and I reached for Robbie, pulling him off the bully. If any neighbors saw this, they would have sworn we jumped our foe. Josh waved his hands frantically from the sidewalk, wailing, "I give, I give."

That day, Robbie became Corey's hero and long-time friend.

Now, he stood next to me, shuddering with sorrow and sniffing like hay fever had gotten the best of him. The thick, cloudy air reminded me of that day Robbie protected him as schoolboys. I thought of the moment I saw him crashing down from my garage. I wasn't there to protect him.

I was hesitant to have friends and other mourners present for Robbie's funeral, knowing El Cucuy was near the burial site. Gertie said we needed to make everything look prim, proper, and original.

Other people I didn't recognize were those who had linked arms or held hands, tears streaming down their faces. The minister offered words of comfort and spoke briefly about the promise of eternal life, emphasizing the hope it brings. He mentioned something about Robbie's commitment to the church and the community, as well as some passages and scriptures I didn't recognize. Unbeknownst to the mourners, a covert operation to snuff out an evil man was unveiled.

I scanned the funeral grounds with a mix of fear, angst, and vigilance. Cire was out there somewhere — I caught a glimpse of him slipping into position behind a line of headstones, his frame blending effortlessly into the shadows. He looked sharp even here, in a dark Bonobos jacket and slim-cut trousers, dressed head-to-toe like any other mourner but wired tight like a hitman waiting for the signal.

Sarya and her team were scattered around the cemetery, all in black, disguised as grieving relatives, their eyes sharp and unblinking. There were more people present than I'd wanted, and I knew some of them were there as decoys.

My prayers were honest, though. I didn't want El Cucuy to turn this into another Sara swim-meet moment. I knew he wanted me, but this — this felt like the perfect stage to send a message back.

Gertie stood next to Alana. They wore stylish, yet classy, wide-brim black hats; only Gertie's black veil distinguished the two. Alana wore dark shades. Sara wore a long, black dress and an overcoat with lace gloves—Chic for a teenager.

"Report status," Gertie whispered in her earpiece.

"Parking lot secure," Jevaun responded.

Another voice chimed, "East perimeter secure."

"Northside clear."

Sarya was holding flowers near a cluster of headstones fifty yards away. "Keep your eyes peeled, Chuck. El Cucuy won't miss a chance like this."

The tension was palpable as the minister concluded his prayer. People placed roses, orchids, and violets on Robbie's casket. Sara put her flower near the head of the casket and leaned in, whispering a prayer. I scanned the area, looking for anything suspicious, as I was the last to place my white rose on Robbie's casket. Kneeling on one knee, I said my goodbyes and promised my brother I would get rid of this El Cucuy.

Turning to hug my wife and daughter, Gertie tapped my shoulder.

"We've got company."

Sal and Radar approached us as the funeral drew to a close. Real and fake hugs were exchanged to maintain the facade. I could sense El Cucuy was around.

Radar nodded. "My condolences."

"Sorry, we're late, Bro," Sal started, trying to hug me. I stiff-armed him. "Wow, really, Chuck?"

"Haven't seen you two in a while." My words jolted with rebellion. "How the fuck did you know Robbie's services were today?"

Both men shrugged. "Eyes in the sky, Chuck," Radar mumbled.

"Whatever, Radar. Sal, this was a private service, so, uh, you two can bounce."

"Hey, I know you're grieving," Sal retorted, "so I'll let this slide. We still need to talk."

Gertie shifted her coat open to reveal her piece. "Sal, you got less than five seconds to disappear."

Both men raised their hands, surrendered, and walked backward to the parking lot. Cire chimed in our ears.

"El Cucuy, 10 o'clock."

We all rotated away from Sal and Radar and gazed to our left. A figure in a dark coat moved at a slow, graceful gait.

Sarya sounded in our ears, "Cire, take this motherfucker out!"

El Cucuy slipped his hand into his pocket, reaching for what we assumed was a weapon, but it looked more like a remote. A shot rang out, echoing through the cemetery.

"Splash," Cire chimed in our earpieces.

As the assassin crumpled to the ground, a deafening explosion shattered the silence to our right. The blast threw us backward a full ten yards. Gertie covered Sara, and Alana fell limp on her side. My vision blurred as I struggled to make sense of what had happened. I couldn't make out what blew up. Sal and Radar disappeared within the plume of smoke, dirt, and rocks. I didn't see either man.

A cacophony of screams filled the burial site. Funeral attendees scattered as tree branches, debris, and blood rained from the sky. Cire and Jevaun were yelling something, but my earpiece was an arm's length away. Sarya and other team members approached the area as people scrambled.

Jevaun made his way to the impact zone in full stride. Cire followed. His face told it all, and he turned away from the carnage. He waved us over to the blast hub. My mind raced. I knew this wasn't an accident. My legs were wobbly, and my eyes widened when I saw the gruesome scene of blood and body parts.

"Is that--"

"It *was* Radar," Jevaun said, covering his nose and mouth. Corey walked up, clutching his chest, gasping for breath, trying to make sense of what transpired. His face was streaked with blood that wasn't his own. Hands trembling, he tried to speak.

Sarya pulled him over to a broken bench from the blast. "He's in shock."

Sirens filled the air as emergency vehicles approached.

"We'll get him some help," I said. "Sounds like we've got more company."

Cire surveyed the blast area as more screams and cries pierced the air. "How do you want to manage this, Bruv?"

Still reeling from the blast, confusion, and chaos, I shook my head. I didn't have an answer. Too many emotions danced within my spirit. Robbie was gone and just laid to rest, while the man who killed him was scrunched over in his own demise.

"Go get whatever you can off El Cucuy and get outta here," I told Cire. "We'll connect later."

Witnessing the additional mayhem hit me. I searched for answers. This was calculated to the letter. As I struggled to process this violent event, I had no other choice but to assume this was part of El Cucuy's plot to take us all out. Radar was in itty-bitty pieces of body matter. He couldn't answer any of my questions, and Sal was likely blown up as well.

"Yo, Jevaun, has anyone seen Sal? He was right next to Radar before the blast."

Jevaun held a shoe in the air. "Is this his? He's probably mixed up in all this shit, fam. Ain't no way he survived this, yo."

Emergency, fire, and police vehicles arrived. They took the necessary steps to secure the area and provide medical assistance to the injured. EMTs wrapped Corey in a thermal shock blanket.

A few cops asked the attendees questions while my favorite detective approached me.

We shook hands. Detective Cravis placed his hands on his hips, surveying the area.

"Lots of shit going on around here, Chuck."

"Detective, I'm only guilty of laying my brother to rest. This chaos happened on its own."

Cravis folded his arms. He continued to survey the area and faced me.

"Look me in my eyes, Chuck. Tell me you had nothing to do with unaliving one of the most notorious human beings on earth."

"Detective, my family, friends, and I were here to say goodbye to my brother."

"Just a pocket full of coincidences, huh, Chuck?"

"What can I say, Detective?"

"A lot, Chuck. If I find out you're tied to any of this, we will have to have a formal conversation. Don't make me put you in cuffs."

I saluted the detective with my index and middle fingers and made my way to my wife and daughter. Sara's face was pale with terror as she gave me a lopsided frown when I asked if she was OK. Alana's eyes were wide with horror, looking at Radar's splattered intestines. The crime scene team captured photos and placed the remains in red plastic bags.

"We have to leave, Chuck."

Alana looked right through me with a stoic gaze. Her words shook me. Three men, including a wicked being, killed her brother-in-law, laid him dead, and blew up no more than fifty yards from where we stood. I knew our marriage wasn't ending, but with everything happening, I did not want to separate from my girls. They were my super glue. I searched the sky - still filled with smoke and ashes - hoping a response would fall from the clouds. I even asked Robbie for words.

"I was thinking the same thing, babe, but we took El Cucuy out. He was responsible for Robbie."

Alana bowed, grabbed my hands, and closed her eyes. She inhaled. I wondered if the metallic scent of smoke and blood disturbed her Zen moment.

"Chuck," she stated. "I need to get Sara away from all of this. I love you. This is a bit much for a teenager."

"Understood."

"You know where I'll be. Call me when all of this is over, and please find JG. Please."

"I will. And what if he contacts you?"

Twisting her lips, Alana looked up and to the left and right. She looked burned out from the events, but still twinkled when she responded.

"If JG contacts me, then I will contact you."

"And I will throw you a party when you come back to me."

Shifting her weight, Alana studied the area behind me. Something distracted her. It was the remembrance of the explosive melee. Many moments ago, two men were walking away from us. Now, ash, sot, and remains, and investigators have occupied the cemetery. If her expressions were a vehicle, it would make several lane changes. "You're more of a partygoer than a party thrower."

"Whatever the case, the party will be for you."

"Why, thank ya kindly," Alana returned with a curtsy.

"If you're going where I think you're going, stop by the storage place. Cash only while you're traveling."

"Sara will love that."

"Let her go crazy in the mall," I suggested. "Just nothing flashy."

Alana laughed - finally. "We're talking about earthtone, Sara."

"Right. What about school?"

"I'll let them know we're away due to a family emergency. It won't be too far from the truth. Bereavement time."

We laughed. It protected the tears.

"Let's get something to eat before you take off."

"Oooh," Alana puckered. "How 'bout that Pinoy barbecue place?"

I thought about our first date when Alana and I ate there. It was a quaint place run by a couple from Cebu City. Alana adored the restaurant. I recall her telling me it reminded her of a place back home with its traditional decor, woven mats, and Filipino artwork. They served marinated, skewered, and grilled pork. I wasn't big on the pig, and they recommended the chicken over rice. Whatever combinations of sauces and ingredients they used, I was hooked.

"Your command is my wish, my dear." I felt comfortable taking my girls out, knowing we were safe from the maniac. I still didn't like the idea of them leaving, but Alana was determined. It seemed too easy to take out El Cucuy, but Gertie was a tactician. She said the plan would work, and it worked.

PIVOT

Mayor Abido's office was large and elegant. For someone not yet thirty, his taste in fine art and design provided a balance of aesthetics, functionality, style, and authority. Everyone who entered his chambers knew he was in charge.

The open-plan office featured a cherry oak desk positioned in front of the ceiling-to-floor windows that faced the city. Minus his laptop, his desk was large enough for three monitors. A framed picture of a family reunion was the sole decor on his desk. The rest were the images of him with various dignitaries, police officers, sports figures, and celebrities hung on the walls, captured on canvas. Most displayed "shake-and-take" poses with individuals giving or receiving plaques, trophies, and certificates. Other photos were side-by-side shots with city officials.

A glass table with mini microphones and coasters for beverages was positioned opposite the mayor's desk. It was large enough for eight people on each side and an open space at the end of the table for his assistant. A leather couch rested next to a striking five-foot granite island with various whiskeys, bourbons, and rum on a tray. The round rug in the center of the office displayed the city's crest. The layout created a welcoming atmosphere for assorted conversations, deals, and negotiations.

The mayor sat sideways in his leather smoker's chair, adjusting the matte black Warby Parker frames perched low on his nose as the Cyphus brothers watched him from across the desk. Charleston, the mayor's brother, leaned against the granite island.

Fidgeting with one of the tassels on his Calvin Klein black-and-white loafers, the mayor finally spoke, his voice measured but carrying weight.

"I have to make a statement about this ruthless mercenary who was shot and then blown up at the city's cemetery. Metro said it looked like a warzone. Luckily, there were only three casualties."

"I saw some of it on the news this morning," the eldest Cyphus brother remarked. "Warzone would define anything El Cucuy is involved in."

Quentin Cyphus inquired, "Why would El Cucuy be here?"

"We'll never know now because he's dead, and I need to let the community know there's nothing to fear."

The mayor continued, "Speaking of fear and safety, have we had any luck whatsoever locating my laptop and/or Mr. Givens?"

"Circumstances like these take time," the Greek gangster stated. "We have people monitoring movements in the city, around his job, and at home. It goes without saying, this is delaying a lot of business and financial transactions."

Preoccupied with his shoe, the mayor chirped, "Bullshit. I can get my guys from the force to monitor movements. I need your people to locate this bastard, and if I were in your betting house, I'd make a large wager that Julius is out of the city—even the country.

"Furthermore," the mayor continued, still focused on his tassel, "I know what it's doing with our business agreement. Business, I agreed only to bail out my brother."

Corey, the older Cyphus brother, cleared his throat as he adjusted his paisley Brioni tie.

"We understand the severity of locating this dipshit nerd. You should be equally concerned, not just for your brother, but for those who you say are on this computer of yours, including us. There is enough evidence to implicate the entire city, including us. Do you understand our position, Mr. Mayor?"

"Spare me the theatrics, Cyphus," the mayor retorted. "I've been involved in larger controversies involving the three-letter agencies and other contingencies, foreign and domestic. If my brother hadn't fucked up, I'd still be overseas getting the best pussy on earth. Let's keep all of this local as we agreed."

Quentin Cyphus pounded the oak desk, "You don't speak like that to my brother! Show some respect!"

The mayor's eyelids raised with surprise. "No disrespect, Quentin. We're all on the same team here. Do you have any ideas, Charlie?"

Charleston dropped a cube of ice in his glass and poured a large portion of Woodford Reserve bourbon. The block clinked the glass as Charleston swirled. He took a sip and winced as the spices and rich flavor burned his throat.

"I got an idea," the mayor's brother snapped. "I'm surprised no one has figured this out yet."

Intrigued by Charleston's notion, the Greek mobsters turned to the back of the room.

"Well, spit it out, Charlie," Mayor Abido commanded. "Haraka! Haraka!"

"Gimme your phone." The mayor's brother pecked at his brother's device with his thumbs like he was playing a video game. He grunted in frustration a few times. Squinting in concentration, he brought the phone closer to his face. He mumbled something about a bypass and a keycode and waited for the phone to respond.

"Damn!"

"What is it?" the older Cyphus brother asked.

Charleston held up his finger. He tapped the phone a few more times and waited. The cell phone beeped three times, and he laughed. "Yeah, bitch! Got your monkey ass!"

Everyone stood to their feet. The mayor folded his fingers close to his chin.

"Where? Where is he, Charlie?"

"Palm Springs. Cali, Mr. Mayor! You probably didn't know you had a location finder on your laptop, didja, Jeffy?"

"Ha! You learn something new every day," the older Greek brother stated.

"Go get that mdudu," the Mayor commanded. "And get my laptop!"

Quentin snapped his fingers and moved his arms like a conductor. "We move methodically and tactfully,"

Charleston responded. "Yeah? What's that mean, Quentin?"

"That means you stay put. We stay put. We'll put a team out there to make sure they return that kleftis. We need locked and secured alibis."

The mayor paced his office. Arms folded, he scratched his sides. Vision tunneling, he asked, "Who took out the high school principal?"

Corey and Quentin turned to Charleston Abido.

"Yo, that wasn't me, Jeffy," he spits. "I thought it was one of your guys from Metro. What's his face?"

"What's his face, Charlie?"

"Ahh, the prince, Jeffy. You're right," Quentin chimed in. "Our man with all the Burger King joints."

The mayor shook his head. "No, I don't get him involved in shit like this. I keep him clean. We need his clean money, influence, and other key players around the city. No, one of my guys from Metro helped me out with the principal. He's a detective."

JULIUS GIVENS

Carrying a Santorini Gyro TO-GO bag, JG walked at a fast pace through Palm Springs' Palm Canyon Drive. The iconic and most popular tourist attraction marked the heart of the downtown desert oasis. With its mid-century architecture, art galleries, and shops, Julius ventured from an Italian bistro with assorted gelato flavors to return to his studio bungalow suite. It would be the perfect evening complement to his gyros from Santorini's.

He loved window shopping and parading in and out of stores and historical venues. He often blended in among the many onlookers along the Walk of Stars, celebrating famous people of the past.

His favorite time away from the bungalow was touring the city and learning about the renowned Black architect Paul R. Williams' designs throughout Palm Springs, which included the Palm Springs Tennis Club, the El Mirador Hotel, which was converted into the Desert Regional Hospital, and a landmarked historical site known as The Center.

Palm Springs was busy, and the bungalow was spacious enough for him to hide in plain sight, overlooking the pool from his private patio. It's where he observed retirees, athletes' wives and girlfriends, and a few celebrities he recognized from TV but couldn't recall their names. The walnut walls in his place were a throwback to the fifties, but uniquely maintained a modern and sophisticated setting. One of the homes reminded him of the Brady Bunch house.

Several weeks have passed since Julius found incriminating material on the mayor's laptop. Several names from the city council, including the city manager, were listed. JG determined these were individuals listed to take the fall; however, other names listed seemed legitimate.

He became more relaxed in his botanical hideaway. Having taken several hikes around the city, he had become accustomed to jogging to Indian Canyon to take his mind off what he called "Black Rose."

Ironically, he met a Wisconsin couple with the same last name, who considered themselves part-time locals. Julius didn't share the commonality, but he gravitated toward the snowbirds who lived in the adjacent bungalow. They knew where to go, what to see, where to eat, and, most importantly, where to isolate in anonymity.

Morning laps in the pool, breakfast on the patio, a walk into town, shopping, then a show or slots at the casino. Golf every Tuesday and Thursday. JG knew the senior Givens' routine because they recalled their entire day to him at dinner. The snowbirds, their routine, and his frequent trail runs provided respite from possessing the mayor's laptop, but he knew this could not last too long. Thinking about the one person who helped him through his mental carnival ride, he sent a text from his burner phone. *Hey. It's JG.*

SOJOURN

We walked out of the Filipino barbecue place full of food and happy to be together. Sara hugged my waist on my right, and my beautiful wife hugged me on my left. It was a proper sending off to safety, solace, and rest for my girls.

"This place hasn't changed in years," I noticed.

"If it ain't broke," Alana retorted.

"True. Do you remember the first time we were here?"

Alana squinted, "It was Martina's 25th birthday. Whew, that was years ago."

I playfully shoulder-check my wife into our daughter, causing them both to stumble and laugh.

"No, silly, I'm talking about the first time you and I came here, like our first date."

"Ooh, Daddy, was I born yet?"

"No, sweetie, your mother and I weren't even a couple yet when we ate here. She wanted to see if I was down for her Pina-pina culture, her people, ya know?"

"And your daddy thought I wouldn't like shrimp and grits or chicken and waffles, but I tore all that up on our next date."

I grabbed Alana close so our daughter wouldn't hear, "and I tore up your special place afterwards."

Alana pushed me and smacked my backside, chuckling, "Get away from me, nasty butt."

"Ew, mom."

"Seriously, sweetie. Get to where you go. Remember, cash only."

Before Alana confirmed my request, her phone chirped.

"Oh, shoot, honey, look. It's JG."

I took the phone and read the message.

"I don't recognize the number," Alana stated. "Do you think it's him?"

I studied the message. "It's likely a prepaid phone. He's a smart guy. He might be using a couple of them."

Alana's forehead wrinkled. "What should I do?"

"Text him back. Ask him if he's OK; if he's safe?"

Alana tapped the message and waited.

"Anything?"

"Nothing. Wait! The bubbles are dancing. He's responding."

"That's a good sign."

"Palm Springs."

"Palm Springs? California?"

"JG always talked about going to see the controversial Marilyn Monroe statue," Alana noted. "I guess that's where he took off to."

"Tell him I can be there in less than two days."

Alana exchanged messages with JG as I contacted Cire, then Jevaun. Cire confirmed and told me Sarya and Gertie were standing by for the next move.

Alana placed the phone to her side. Her long breaths indicated something was wrong.

"Julius said before he switched out phones, he had several messages from Detective Cravis. The police found a dead body in his backyard and were calling him for questions. It's looking like he's on the run for killing a man, not discovering illegal activity on the mayor's computer."

SPLASH

"The mayor's covering up his tracks," I responded. "They're definitely trying to set him up. I gotta get to JG before they do."

Alana's nose scrunched. She struggled to ask her question. She squinted and blurted, "But who would know his whereabouts? You just said he's smart by using a prepaid phone, so he's being careful. Right? Right?"

I held out my arms for Alana to walk into. She was getting emotional, and I reassured her JG would return from Palm Springs in one piece and alive.

"He's probably a big bag of nerves out there, Chuck. Please help him."

I kissed Sara on her nose, then her forehead. I instructed her to stay close to her mom and not to spend too much while she's away. I repeated my kissing ritual with Alana and said, "Maybe I should check out that Marilyn Monroe statue while I'm there, you know, to see what the fuss is about."

ILL-TIMED

The slender man approached the resort lobby wearing all white. The outfit was a single color, black, with Dolce & Gabbana lettering across the neckline and black Portofino D&G low-top sneakers. The short sleeves hugged his muscular biceps, and the striations in his forearms were visible; he frequently used his hands.

He removed his aviator glasses and gave the young concierge a Hollywood, flirtatious smile. He waited for a beat for the exotic pheromones from his Tom Ford Oud Wood perfume to overwhelm the young worker. It was a lost cause, and she would have given him her Social Security number if he had requested it. Instead, he asked for the room number of his relatives. Last name: Givens.

The young concierge was flustered by the svelte gent's disposition and the four one-hundred-dollar bills he handed her. She mentioned that the Givens were considered private clients, but she'd do it for him.

"You're the best," he said, handing her another C-note. "I hope you're a secret-keeper."

Astonished by the generous tip, she shoved the money in her slacks and told him, "Your secret is safe with me. Bungalow 408."

He tapped the information into his phone and walked through the resort's common area. Toddlers played on a splash pad with their mothers while teenagers ran up three flights to a towering waterslide. He moved with purpose around the fitness center and lap pool and saw the sign for Bungalows 400 to 410. He surveyed the area for traffic and made his way to 408.

He knocked three times and waited.

The door opened, and the elderly couple was standing at the threshold, confused, not expecting visitors.

"Can I help you, son?"

The man's eyes narrowed. "I'm not your son. Where is Julius Givens?"

Mr. Givens' face was etched with uncertainty, and he frowned at his wife. "I'm sorry. We're the Givens, but we don't know anyone by that name," the man said.

"Who are you looking for?" Mrs. Givens asked.

"Julius. Givens."

"You have the wrong bungalow, sir," Mr. Givens stated. "This is practically our home away from home, and we always stay in this cottage."

The man pushed Mr. Givens aside and closed the door. "I'm going to give you to the count of three to tell me where Julius Givens is." He pulled out a Banish .22 with a rimfire silencer attached.

"Oh, my Lord," Mrs. Givens shouted. "We don't know anyone named Julius, sir. Please, you have to believe us."

"One."

"Please, we don't know the person you are asking about, like my wife said. We're snowbirds. We're on vacation!"

"Two."

"Please. Please," the woman cried. She was standing behind her husband, gripping his arm. "We're the Givens from Wisconsin."

"Three."

"Wait!" The husband shouted. "There's a new guy--"

The silencer zipped twice and then again twice more. The sound from the TV and the faint hum of the air conditioner remained. The assassin stood still for a moment, scanning the area. He inhaled for a beat and searched the bungalow for the mayor's laptop.

He stepped over the motionless couple. Their faces frozen in terror and bewilderment. He didn't want to take them out, but he had a job to do. He gazed at the man for a moment, wondering what the old fart was about to say. Stepping back over the couple, he swept the area, only to determine the laptop wasn't there.

The hitman checked his watch and tapped a message on his phone. He moved swiftly, wiping down any surfaces before he quietly exited the place. The door clicked shut, and he made his way back through the recreation area. He ventured over to a wine and cheese reception by the pool. He blended in perfectly, engaging in small talk with a group of women wearing tropical printed swimsuits. They eyed the assassin and asked him to stick around for some fun. He flashed his million-dollar smile and declined before disappearing into the garden.

The next morning, Julius sat on his patio to enjoy his strawberry-banana-blueberry smoothie. He didn't see the Givens doing their laps at the pool. He didn't let it concern him as they were likely taking a walk or altering their routine.

Within minutes, two golf carts with resort security escorted three police officers past Julius' patio next to the Givens. More officers arrived, and detectives in plainclothes followed. Then the coroner arrived. Crime scene tape surrounded Bungalow 408.

"Oh snap," JG mumbled. He hurdled over the patio and jogged to the lobby. Bystanders and observers buzzed as detectives interviewed the guests. Staff members were crying and hugging each other while a female police officer questioned the concierge.

JG tapped a valet on the shoulder, "What happened?"

"Bro! The Givens got murked last night."

"What?"

"One of our long-time, favorite guests from Wisconsin was shot and killed in their bungalow. Man, I'm gonna miss those fat tips."

JG turned to stone.

"Dude, you look like you just saw a ghost," the valet said.

"I can't believe it," JG muttered. "I just saw them."

"Did you know the Givens?"

"I, I didn't," JG lied. "Excuse me."

JG ran from the resort, past the upscale boutiques, bumping people without apology and toward the canyon. He didn't know where to find refuge. The bungalow may no longer be safe. Was it a coincidence?

DIFFERENCES

The hitman approached the top steps of the rooftop. The sun was setting over Palm Springs. A warm, orange glow cast a tranquil hue across the city. He stared at the highest peak of a mountain and wondered if anyone had attempted to hike that far.

A few minutes passed, and the door to the rooftop opened. An imposing figure wearing Oliver Peoples wire-framed glasses approached. His expressionless face told the assassin nothing. He put his hand inside his tailored suit jacket, and the hitman flinched. The boss pulled out a tin can of strawberry Altoids and plucked three into his mouth.

"What happened?" the boss asked, his voice low and controlled.

The hitman shook his head. "I don't make mistakes; let's establish that. I asked for Givens and got an old couple's room from Nebraska or Wisconsin. They could have been hiding Julius, so I clipped them."

The boss's eyes narrowed. He shifted his weight and tossed two more mints in his mouth, waiting for the hitman to continue.

"I got the wrong room, and Julius is still out there with the laptop."

The boss walked alongside the hitman and looked out at the horizon. He let out a slow, measured breath. "This is a serious setback, Murdock. We can't afford for Julius to escape—that laptop. We need him and ensure he doesn't have any copies. You won't get another chance."

The hitman swallowed. "I'll find him, Detective Cravis."

WAYFARING

Jevaun pulled up to my house in a custom Mercedes Sprinter Van. Cire, Sarya, and I were waiting with our gear. Dirty Gertie was going to stay close to home and keep her eyes on the club. Hospital night was one of the most popular themed nights at the club, and Gertie knew the mayor would be there.

Cire took the passenger's seat. I opened the sliding door for Sarya, and we hopped in the back. "Daaaaang, Jevaun, this is nice," Sarya complimented.

"Yo, we need a lil' suttin-suttin' to keep us comfy for our road trip, right?" No one disagreed with the plush captain's chairs and mini sofa. It could easily seat ten adults.

Pushing buttons and fidgeting with the recliner, Sarya said, "Gert's gonna be mad she missed all this."

Cire sucked his teeth. "She can't puff in here, sis. That's why she didn't take the road trip." We laughed at Cire's truth. Gertie wouldn't last two hours without her cannabis.

The drive to Palm Springs was relaxing. Jevaun gave us the two-hour mark. I received a text from JG. *They're here. Plz help!*

I texted our ETA, and he sent a news alert: "Elderly couple found dead at Palm Springs resort. Suspected foul play."

They stayed next door. Last name Givens.

"Shit!"

"What's up?" Sarya asked.

She read the news alert on my phone. "Do you think it's connected?"

"Oh, it's connected. We gotta get to JG before it's too late."

Jevaun accelerated the Sprinter. He understood the assignment. There was no telling what would happen if the mayor's goons got their hands on JG.

"How'd they find him so fast?" Jevaun asked as he switched lanes.

"It's hard to say, Jevaun. I don't know if they tracked his phone or,"

"They tracked the laptop," Sarya snapped.

Cire spun in his captain's chair and faced us. "Rassclot! I didn't know that was even possible, Bruv."

Sarya exchanged a worried glance with me and Cire. She wasn't concerned about what or who we would encounter. She didn't want to be too late.

Passing through the Riverside area, we drew closer to the city and planned our approach. Jevaun concealed our arsenal within the vehicle's panels. Sarya grabbed the Smith & Wesson nine-millimeter. She looked down at the barrel and inspected the chamber.

Though the best sharpshooter on the planet, Cire pulled out a Leupold Delta Point Pro with a laser.

"I take it you don't plan on missing, Cire."

Cire sucked his teeth. "I never do."

Jevaun chimed in, "We've got reinforcements nearby in Cathedral City. It's mad close to where we'll be, and my dude Marcus and his lady are scouting the area."

Sarya spun in her seat until it clicked into place. "I hope these people don't get all twisted when they see a bunch of Black folks around this place."

Keeping his eyes on the road, Jevaun retorted, "You can take the girl out of Chester. I know you and Gertie are mad busy with your sex spot and all that, but look up Section 14 on your phone. Palm Springs has more Black history and businesses that would surprise a lot of folks."

"I'm saying," Sarya volleyed, "leave what Gert and I do outta your mouth. That's our covert cover, and secondly, I'm from Chester, mother-phuggin, pee-aye. I don't know much about these bougie West Coast resorts. When I travel, I flow to where my people are. Grenada. Zanzibar, Cabo Verde. Trinidad."

"Yeah, Bruv," Cire joked. "She goes where her people are."

"Alright, it's time," I redirect my team. As the sun hid behind the desert horizon, I reminded everyone of their assignments and the mission: secure JG and the laptop to safety, avoid the local authorities, and get out of town without making a splash.

My phone buzzed.

Marilyn Monroe statue. Downtown Park.

"Time to move. JG just hit me."

ELUDING

Julius glanced, paranoid at every sound and passing car. Even the rustling of the palm leaves above made him jumpy. The weight of the 16-inch laptop was only four pounds, but it felt like twenty. The warm wind cooled his nerves and dried his linen shirt and pants. His tan Polo bear baseball cap was soaked at the brim, and JG's tan Nike Air Max 270s appeared brown from perspiration, too.

He walked on North Palm Canyon Drive towards the statue. Several tourists stood by, under, and next to the 26-foot statue, capturing photos and videos. Two figures emerged from the shadows behind JG. He couldn't stop or he'd be caught. The men walked with a purpose and moved past the crowd with boldness-not caring if they bumped an elderly person or kicked a stroller. They kept JG in their sight.

A few more paces, JG ducked into a home decor boutique. The men followed. Inside, JG moved around the store, observing fun-looking designs of moons, geckos, colorful elephants in bathtubs, and other eclectic, metal art. He peeked left and right among the ornaments and dipped in and out of the aisles, doing his best to avoid being snatched by the two men. He hid behind a six-foot peacock in the train display, and he felt hidden and secure. JG heard the men fussing about losing him.

"He was right over there by those painted lizards," Murdock conveyed. "He can't be too far; let's go!"

JG sent another text. *2 men. Help!* He darted through the streets, past various shops and restaurants. Heart pounding, he passed the towering figure of Marilyn twice and entered a burger spot. The two men were relentless in their pursuit and walked past the burger spot.

"Can I help ya, sugar?"

A young greeter with cinnamon skin tapped Julius's elbow. She wore a purple t-shirt with K-Jay's Burgers stretched across her top, thanks to her large breasts. She wore blue jeans one size too small for her curvy, apple-shaped bottom, and her sneakers matched her shirt. Her bright, welcoming smile and cheerful vibe comforted JG. He forgot people were trying to kill him.

"Uh, yes. Wait, no. I'm waiting, can I sit back there?

With her cheerful attitude, she smiled and scribbled on her notepad.

"Sure. I'll put the Gatlins at the next booth. You sit right over there, and I'll get you a glass of water. Do you want lemons?"

JG nodded and tapped his phone while studying the front door.

K-Jay's Burgers. Last booth on the right.

"JG is in K-Jay's Burgers," I said into my comms. "I'm heading there. Close in and keep your eyes open."

Cire responded, "I'm on the roof."

"Sarya's on the bench next to Marilyn," Jevaun stated. "We've got less than five minutes before this goes sideways."

I walked to the burger spot and headed to JG. The restaurant was buzzing with chatter, clinking silverware, and vibrant noise. *'Where I'm From'* by the Digable Planets played in the background.

"How ya feeling, JG?" I asked.

"A helluva lot better now that you're here. You're bigger than I expected. Alana never said you were a big guy."

"Meh, it's the shirt," I joked. "Let's get you outta here before those bad guys show up."

JG's eyes darted nervously to the door like he saw a ghost. He slid down in the booth. "It's them, it's them."

"OK,' I said calmly. "You saw them before they saw you, so it's cool. Just stay low. Get under the table if you can."

"What?"

"Get under the table."

The two men walked around the burger spot searching for JG, ignoring the cute greeter's request to wait to be seated. The slender man approached the table, not noticing JG. Our eyes met, and the staring contest began. I broke the trance.

"So do you want my phone number or something?"

"Where did you find that messenger bag?" the man asked.

"Belongs to a friend of mine. What's your name?" I pulled the bag closer to me.

"Murdock. Where's your friend now?" the thin-framed man inquired.

"Went to hit the head." Murdock's partner appeared. He cracked his knuckles, his imposing frame enough to intimidate anyone into compliance. He didn't scare me.

"Gimme dat bag before you get tossed across these tables," the big guy ordered.

"And ruin everyone's dinner? Let's not do that."

The two men grabbed me out of the booth, exposing JG hiding under the table. I held onto the messenger bag. I stood, tussling with the men, trying to hide JG. I shoved Murdock into the kitchen doors, creating a crashing sound. The restaurant fell silent, and eyes turned to the confrontation. Cell phones out, including a plump redhead in a pink *I Luv Palm Springs* t-shirt in the neighboring booth. The big man noticed JG on the floor.

"There's that motherfu -" the big man stopped mid-sentence. His face twisted, frozen in time, and he crashed to the floor. Behind him was the cute, perky waitress holding a taser.

A celebratory roar erupted throughout the restaurant. The vibrant smile returned on the greeter's face as she threw her hands up in victory. A few tourists gave her high fives.

Murdock pushed through the kitchen door, face painted with anger. His clothes were stained with burger grease. "Imma need that bag, bro."

"You might want to bounce, Murdock," I advised. "Whatever your intention, it ain't gonna fly. Look around at all these witnesses. Hell, we're probably live and trending now."

"Fuck! Cravis is going to kill me." Murdock smacked the cell phone from the redhead's hand. People gasped. He pushed past the other restaurant goers out the door and into the cool night air. JG made his way next to me. I spoke into the comms to the crew.

"Jevaun, come drag this gorilla out of the restaurant," I requested. "Sarya, keep your eyes on the dirty guy leaving the restaurant. He's our hitman."

Cire crackled in my ear. "I could easily clip him, Chuck."

"No. Track him down. He'll lead us to . . ."

"Chuck, you broke up, Bruv."

I couldn't believe what I heard. I turned to JG. "Did I hear Murdock say the name, 'Cravis'?"

JG shrugged. "Could've been," he said, flicking a piece of food off his shoulder. "It sounded like Davis or Mavis, but now that you mentioned it, Cravis could have been it. Do you know who he's talking about?"

Lost in thought, I searched for a reason why the detective would be drawn into this.

"Alright, let's get to the sprinter so we can ask this big mofo some questions."

"Sarya?"

"What's up, Chuck?"

"Snatch this Murdock guy, and we'll meet you in the sprinter. Cire is close."

"I see him," Sarya huffed in her mouthpiece. She weaved her way through the crowd and the tourists. The scent of food and summer air blended uncannily. She locked in on Murdock as he darted through a sea of people, just out of reach. His pace was steady, giving no indication that he was being followed.

He looked back at Sarya, who tilted her head towards a store. They walked a few yards in front of a parade, and Murdock crossed the street. Sarya stayed with him. Murdock glanced over his shoulder. His eyes glazed with anxiety as he saw Sarya close. Too close. He pushed past a man, nearly knocking over a street performer drumming on Lowe's buckets.

Sarya quickened her pace, determined to catch up to Murdock. A family of 15 wearing blue *Clark Family Reunion* shirts blocked the sidewalk. They asked Sarya for her help with a group photo. She watched the man disappear into the crowd.

Clicking the Canon Rebel multiple times, she waved, sidestepped the family, and ran the next two blocks. Just as she was about to radio that she lost Murdock, she saw him turn the corner. Her heart skipped a beat as she followed him. Murdock skipped over some bushes and ran down an alley.

Sarya saw Murdock skid to a halt in the alley. Blocking him was Cire. He was holding a black, chrome Sig Sauer P320 9mm. That piece brought heat.

Cire's voice calmed the chaos. "You're coming with us, Bruv."

Murdock didn't resist. His shoulders slumped in defeat. Sarya approached from behind, patting him down for weapons. Cire took Murdock by the arm, and Sarya followed. He didn't resist. They led him back down the alley as a sleek black Mercedes Sprinter waited, the engine idling.

Murdock shook his head, mumbling, "All this because of the fucking Givens from Wisconsin."

Cire opened the doors and pushed Murdock inside. He stumbled over his counterpart and fell at JG's feet. JG switched seats next to me. Securing both men with zip ties, Cire hopped inside and slid the door closed. He sucked his teeth and moved to the front of the sprinter.

Sarya let out a sigh of relief. Jevaun pulled off and said, "My peeps are waiting for us in Cathedral City, Chuck."

"I'll see you next time, Marilyn. On to Cathedral City."

We drove through the gated community and took a few turns. Some of the homes epitomized luxury living. Without a doubt, entertainers and sports figures resided here. Cire whistled as we passed a house with a large RV settled in its own parking space. One home resembled a paradise oasis with several water features cascading off rocks.

Marcus Jackson's three-car garage was large enough for the sprinter. It was already open when we pulled up. Jevaun tapped the rear-view mirror, and the garage closed. We brought the two men to the edge of the sprinter and waited for Marcus.

I pointed at the slender man. "Your name is Murdock. We've established that. What's your name, big fella?"

"Stacy," the big man huffed.

"Well, Stacy and Murdock," I turned, "I don't know how the rest of this evening is going to go. But it's up to you because, well, I'm in one of those moods."

Cire huffed. "Aw, shit, Bruv, really? Can we find out if Marcus' wife cooked something first? I'm famished."

"Follow me," Jevaun ordered, "and yes, she cooked, bro."

Sarya, JG, and Cire went inside the house, leaving me with two roughnecks. I stood, rubbing my hands together, unravelling all that transpired. I, too, was famished, but I had questions.

I stood in front of Murdock.

"How you answer this question determines if I put you and your buddy, Stacy, in a hole out here."

Murdock looked at Stacy and over to me. "What's up?"

I made prayer hands under my chin.

"How do you know Detective Gene Cravis?

"Don't say shit, Murdock!" Stacy yelled.

With a quick, forceful motion, I clapped my hands around Stacy's ears, dropping him to his knees.

"Yo!" Murdock yelled. "The fuck, man. I'll tell you."

Arms folded, watching Stacy writhe in pain, I asked again. "How do you know Detective Gene Cravis? Cravis from Metro."

"I take care of things for him."

"Things like the old couple at the resort?"

Murdock inhaled. "That was an accident."

"Was it? What if JG was in the room?"

"He would've murked his ass," Stacy barked. I followed with a left jab to his solar plexus, so he would lean into my right cross to his temple, sending Stacy to sleep.

Squirming, Murdock lost all toughness. "Yo, I told you I would answer your questions."

"Talk."

Murdock said he was sent to Palm Springs to scare JG into handing over the laptop. Detective Cravis told him JG stumbled across something explosive on the mayor's laptop, evidence that could bring down the most powerful men in the city. They were sure that the evidence involved the Cyphus Brothers, and it was the brothers who wanted JG to disappear.

"So Cravis is on the Cyphus Brothers' payroll?" I asked.

"Cravis is about his guacamole," Murdock said matter-of-factly.

"How did they know JG was here?"

"Tracker."

"Of course," I plucked the air. "A damned tracker."

"It sent me right to him," Murdock said.

"Not quite," I retorted.

"You know what I mean. We knew he was here and not at his house."

"I'm assuming Cravis is expecting your call," I noted.

Murdock's face twisted. "I'm supposed to meet him on one of the resort roofs with JG and the laptop."

"And this guy," I said, pointing to the big guy I knocked out.

"Just backup for guys like you."

"You need better backup, fam."

CONFRONTATIONS

The night air reminded me of why many people enjoyed vacationing in California. Just a hint of coolness, but comfortable enough not to worry about a jacket.

I led Murdock up the steps with a firm grip, despite the zip ties serving as additional resistance. Even with JG and the laptop safe, I knew this wasn't over —especially with Cravis behind it. Lies and deceit. He had the means and resources to spin this to his advantage. He had the Cyphus Brothers' muscle and the mayor's support. If anything, this rooftop meeting was the perfect space to take me out.

We got to the top of the rooftop. Our shoes crunched on the gravel. My eyes scanned the area, noticing stones and tar buckets in the corners. Air conditioning units and tunnel vents decorated the rest of the roof. I told Murdock to sit in front of the door and wait for Cravis to appear.

"You're not that smart," Murdock suggested. He held his bound hands in the air. "If Cravis sees me sitting here with these ties around my wrists, he's going to know something's up."

He was right, and I couldn't risk Cravis putting a bullet into Murdock's head. I clipped the hard plastic. Murdock massaged his wrist and shook them to gain circulation.

"You do something stupid, I swear I'll take you out," I warned, exposing my 9mm.

"It's going to look weird to me just sitting here."

"Tell him you're resting your legs."

I heard steps approaching the rooftop door, and I made my way behind one of the AC units.

Detective Cravis walked through the door carrying his suit jacket. His shoulder holster was residing on the right side, indicating Gene was left-handed. I don't think I ever paid attention. Wearing his wire-frame glasses, his eyes flickered as he saw Murdock sitting down.

"What are you doing? Where's JG, and where's the laptop?"

"Shit got twisted," Murdock said, "but hear me out, man, I have a plan. I know where he is."

The detective shifted his weight. Shaking his head, he took his glasses off and massaged his forehead. "You're out of time, and I'm out of options, Murdock. What the fuck is going on?"

"Cravis!" I called out behind the big vent.

His face was masked with calm, but his eyes displayed complete surprise as I walked from the metal vents. He chuckled, a low, menacing grunt. "You're just a big bag of coincidences, huh, Chuck? What are the odds? Like, seriously, what are you doing here?"

"I came to see the Marilyn Monroe statue and bumped into your guy Murdock," I quipped. "Who would know we know the same people?"

Cravis forced a smile and shifted his smirk to a converted frown. "You're out of your league, Chuck. You don't quite understand the big picture. You're interfering in police business."

"Oh, you have jurisdiction in Palm Springs now?"

The detective took a deep breath. It reminded me of Alana and her moments of seeking Zen. I suddenly missed my wife and daughter. Cravis casually slid his hands in his Athletic Fit pants.

"There are powerful people with powerful friends even in Palm Springs, and they won't hesitate to protect each other."

"Meaning, you're willing to kill for it?"

The detective's eyes narrowed as he took another breath before he laughed. "Do you forget who you're talking to? I know you're responsible for several bodies in our city morgue. You and your team. C'mon, Chucky, sometimes, sacrifices must be made."

Before I could respond, Murdock made a sudden move for the rooftop exit. Cravis pulled his piece from his holster, turned, and pulled the trigger once. Murdock fell face-first. He wasn't moving.

My heart raced and lunged toward Cravis, knocking the gun from his hand. It skittered across the gravel. Cravis bent down to pull his .22 from his ankle. I caught the detective's hand and twisted it. Cravis growled in pain and threw a wild punch. I ducked and drove my knee into his ribs. Without hesitation, I wrenched his arm, spinning him off balance, and delivered a Mike Tyson blow to his jaw. Cravis collapsed against the tar buckets.

"You should have stayed out of this, Chuck!"

"Probably," I responded, "but I made a promise."

"Do you think this changes anything?" Cravis said, staggering to his feet. "The mayor will still come after JG until he gets that laptop. You can't protect him forever."

"Don't have to. Just long enough to put your dirty ass away."

The night air cooled. The city lights below seemed distant. Detective Cravis and I locked eyes. My mind raced. I've done some wild shit in my life, but standing in front of a dirty cop who was protecting a dirty mayor and dirty city officials was another level. We stood in silence for a moment, contemplating our next move.

Cravis charged me with flying fists. I met him head-on, where we became lightweight sumo wrestlers, grappling and trying to gain the upper hand on each other - on the rooftop of our battleground. I knew the detective still had his .22 in his ankle holster, so my objective was not to get shot.

I provided a right hook to his ribs that I knew would ache in the morning. I threw two more combinations to the detective's ribs that crippled him. Cravis recovered with a lunging punch to my midsection, which I wasn't prepared for, and staggered me. I was gasping for breath when the detective took the opportunity to go for his weapon again.

A shadow moved in the corner of the roof. I turned just in time to see Murdock with Cravis' gun in his hand. His torso blood-soaked, he approached us.

"Murdock, don't," I shouted.

Murdock's eyes were filled with rage. "Fuck you, man, and fuck you, Cravis!"

Cravis now had his backup weapon, but he feared the hitman. "Look, Murdock, there's a lot of money waiting for you. I've always taken care of you. We had a deal."

Murdock shook his head, "Not anymore."

"So, you're just going to shoot me? I'm a –"

The shot came before Cravis finished. In a swift motion, Murdock pulled the trigger. Cravis fired back at Murdock. The deafening cracks of simultaneous gunshots split the air.

Murdock's eyes widened in shock. The detective's bullet hit him square in the chest. He struggled for air and coughed blood before he crumpled to his knees. Tears flowed, and he fell dead to his side.

I looked over to Cravis. He was leaning on the rooftop's edge. He gasped a few times, also struggling with his breathing as he let the pistol fall to his side. I couldn't tell where he was shot, but he was hurting. He staggered, holding his midsection, and toppled backward, disappearing over the edge. The sickening thud hitting the pavement below was met with screams and terror from vacationers.

Cire made it up to the rooftop, holding his piece.

"You good, Bruv?"

Surveying the area, I looked back at Murdock. There was something about him that had some good in him. He could have killed me and dealt with Cravis on his terms. Cire and I looked over the rooftop. A small gathering of people was assembling, pointing and screaming at the dead body.

"We gotta roll, Bruv," Cire commanded.

AFTERMATH

We piled back into the Sprinter and headed home. Jevaun and the crew left Stacy on the Palm Springs roof next to a dead Murdock.

I told JG he'd still need to lay low, but I'd keep the laptop. He had no problems handing me the messenger bag. Sarya sat in the row by herself, arms folded and pouting.

"Something the matter?"

Sarya gave me a stiff jab to my shoulder. It was a good one. Good enough for me to grab my arm, "Ow!"

"Your ass could've died on that rooftop, Chuck," Sarya proclaimed. "We work as a team. You didn't bring me and Jevaun out here to barbecue with Jevaun's people."

"Cire was close," I mentioned.

"But not close enough. You had a fuckin' hitman and a dirty cop up there. Anything could have happened."

Jevaun chimed in, "She's right, Chuck. Anything could've happened up there, fam. You can't be pulling that selfish shit way out here in Cali, yo. This ain't our turf."

"Everybody's right," I said. "Let's get home and regroup. Can any of you think of somebody inside Metro who might not be linked to the mayor, the Cyphus brothers, or any of this corrupt shit?"

The sprinter fell silent. JG turned to Sarya. "I can do a cross-reference from the file on the laptop to determine what cops aren't listed."

"Yeah, but just because they ain't in those tabs, doesn't mean they ain't dirty," Sarya responded.

JG waved his hand. "Trust me. If anyone from Metro PD is involved, they're on the list or vice versa."

"Save your time, Bruv," Cire interrupted. "I know who we can chop it up with."

"When did you become pals with Metro?" Jevaun asked.

Cire sucked his teeth and held up two fingers. "Two things. 'Your network is your net worth' and 'it's not what you know, it's who you know."

"So, who do you know, Cire?" Sarya snapped. "What's his name?"

"*Her* name is Leticia Rankin, and she's perfect for this. She handles financial crimes, identity theft, and embezzlement."

Sarya smacked her forehead. "Why didn't I know it was a shorty? That thing is going to fall off if you keep putting it in the wrong places."

"Whatever, Rah," Cire said. "This is a working, professional relationship with a credible detective."

"Uh-huh. Don't let Gertie find out," Sarya joked.

"You two are like eighth graders," I interrupted. "Let's get everyone situated and refreshed. Cire, reach out to the detective and let her know we'll meet her first thing in the morning."

"Say less, Bruv, I'm on it."

The last time I was in Metro's police department, we learned JG was missing. It was also the last time Sal was with us. Shit got really weird with Sal. I missed the guy.

We walked through the sterile hallway as the front desk clerk directed us. There was a harsh glow on me and Cire as we passed plain-clothed and uniformed officers. Some moved with purpose and hurried between desks, other offices, and interrogation rooms. One cop was on level twelve of Tetris. One blonde-haired detective chomped on a bear claw and slowed his pace to ask if we knew where we were going. Coordinated, we pointed to the office in front of us.

Detective Leticia Rankin's office was small, cluttered with papers, files stacked haphazardly in a corner cabinet, and on her desk. A bulletin board displayed photos, notes, and a map of the city with markings. A list of every bank in the town occupied another stick pad on the wall.

She was an attractive woman with sharp features and a confident demeanor. She shopped at Ann Taylor. I recognized the blouse I purchased for my wife. Her dark, wavy hair was pulled back into a neat ponytail, and her piercing gaze took everything in at once.

"Cire," she said with a hint of warmth in her voice. "It's been a while."

Cire smiled with a hint of nostalgia in his eyes. He extended his hand to shake. "Leticia. Um, Detective Rankin. Good to see you."

I noticed the subtle exchange between them. There was more history to what Cire led on to be; something unspoken but palpable. I'd have to rib Cire about it later. We needed to focus on the task at hand.

"Detective Rankin," I began, "we need to talk to you about Detective Cravis."

Rankin's expression hardened. She snapped into a professional poise. "Gene? What about him?"

I took a deep breath, recalling the events that led to the rooftop. "Cravis is dirty. Was dirty. He hired a hitman named Murdock to eliminate Julius Givens, who had incriminating evidence against the mayor and many others. We managed to get JG, uh, Mr. Givens to safety, but Cravis and Murdock found him in Palm Springs."

Rankin found her seat. She folded her legs and her arms as she listened. I can tell her mind was racing, processing. "And you expect me to believe the mayor is involved in this? How?"

I leaned forward, palms up. "I know it sounds far-fetched, but it's the truth. The mayor has powerful connections due to his previous job in Africa. He's willing to do whatever it takes to protect himself and those listed in the files. We're pretty sure he's connected to the Cyphus Brothers as well."

Rankin looked at Cire. His eyes told her I wasn't lying. She sighed and asked, "What happened on the roof in Palm Springs?"

"We were able to capture Murdock at a burger spot. We learned he was linked to Cravis because he mentioned Cravis was going to kill him for not completing the mission. I took him on the roof with me to confront Cravis. We fought, and I knocked the gun away from him, but Murdock got it."

"Cravis had a backup on his ankle, and they turned on each other. Murdock said something about being double-crossed and shot Cravis. Cravis got one off at Murdock, too."

Rankin listened and tapped her pen against the table, deep in thought. She nodded.

"Anything else?"

I shrugged. "There's a big statue of Marilyn Monroe in the middle of the street there."

"Where is this JG guy?"

Cire chimed in, "He's somewhere safe until all this blows over."

Rankin smiled at Cire's comments. She stood up and looked at me with a stern grimace. "Gene. Gene's been the type of cop who makes friends with the wrong people even if it's to solve a case," she said.

"We, uh, worked together maybe four or five years ago," she continued, "maybe longer. Right after the COVID pandemic. Joint task force. He insisted on taking the lead when it was clearly our show. I didn't care as long as we got the bastards, but everything felt shady about the case for a long time."

Cire asked, "What happened?"

We could see the pain of the past revisit Detective Rankin. She tried to speak. She shook her head at whatever memory still haunted her. She walked past us, closed her door, and faced us.

"Alright, no one, and I mean no one else from Metro gets involved. We don't know who we can trust anyway."

"That's why we came to you," Cire said.

"You've got my attention," Rankin responded. "Keep this JG fella safe, and we'll take care of these dirty bastards. Thanks for coming in, guys, seriously."

We shook hands, and I noticed Cire watching Rankin with a mixture of admiration and something deeper. As we left the office, I nudged him.

"Keeping secrets?"

We drove back to my house listening to Alex Isley. *Good and Plenty* was playing. It took about ten minutes before Cire said anything.

"I never figured out how you could be with one person, let alone be married, given how much dangerous shit we do, Bruv."

I let him speak.

"I met Leticia after one of our missions. I want to say it was around the time of the joint operation she had with Cravis and his team. I knew him from somewhere, but it wasn't until she recalled the story, ya know?"

"Sure."

"Anyway," Cire continued, "I knew she was a cop and, shit, Bruv. Me and the cops never mixed, not even when I was with MPs, ya know?"

I nodded.

"Our energy was explosive, and the sex was crazy passionate, Bruv. She was a firecracker," he said, recounting something amusing.

"She was headstrong on knowing what I did, and I couldn't tell her. I thought explaining that I was in the military would cease the questions, but she kept mashing me, Bruv. I didn't know what to do. I liked her, ya know? Like what you and Alana have, ya know?"

"Oh, shit, Cire! For real?"

"Yah, Bruv. I never felt that good. We could do anything together. Well-rounded and loved both American and international football. Then, our team embarked on a few missions abroad, and the connection between us began to fade. I was surprised she agreed to meet us today, to be honest."

I shook my head. "No matter your memories of each other, let's count this as a victory that we have someone on the inside."

"Of course, Bruv."

"And," I continued, "like Sarya said, Gertie will kill you."

"Speaking of Sarya," Cire said, "how's that been working so close to your old flame?"

"Like jumping out of a perfect plane with no parachute."

DEVIATION

The mayor walked through his chambers, checking his Fitbit after his morning jog. He grabbed his jump rope and skipped for seventeen minutes. Dripping wet, he dropped to the floor and did seventy-five push-ups at an expedient pace.

He maneuvered into a cat-cow yoga pose and went into various warrior poses, followed by a downward-facing dog. He held that pose the longest with syncopated breathing.

Checking his watch again, he stripped naked and walked into the sauna. He set the timer for 10 minutes. The buzzer sounded, and the mayor walked into his shower. The hot water created additional steam. As the mayor lathered, the glass door opened.

"Right on time," he said.

A pair of hands found the mayor's waist, fingers tracing his skin. A brown-skinned frame pressed against the mayor. He looked down at the tiles and complimented her decorated toenails. Water sliding between their bodies, he pressed his lips against hers and reached between her cheeks.

Her breath paused before she moaned as he caressed her. The steam thickened, blurring everything but the feel of each other. Skin on skin, they moved and swayed in various positions. She dug her nails into the mayor's back. He smacked her butt.

"Take care of me," he demanded. She got on her knees and did what he asked her to do. Another buzzer sounded four minutes later. The mayor stepped out of the shower, leaving her alone.

He opted for his tailored charcoal Brioni suit, white shirt, and black Tom Ford tie. He walked out to his office to find his breakfast and a green smoothie waiting at the conference table.

His executive assistant appeared with his cell phone, two newspapers, a tablet, and an envelope of cash. The mayor thanked her and excused her.

While he sipped his green smoothie, the brown frame appeared from his bathroom. She was wearing a fitted Actively Black cropped tee and high-waisted leggings. She read a message from her Apple watch and tapped the face as she approached the mayor.

He smacked her bottom and grabbed her close to him for a passionate kiss. She smiled and held out her hand. The mayor placed the envelope in her hand and told her, "I'll see you in a week." She blew him a kiss, took a piece of his bacon, and left.

"Sorry to bother you, Mayor," his assistant said through the intercom, "but there's an urgent call for you on two."

He stood, adjusting his jacket and tie, and walked over to his desk. He planted his feet at shoulder's length apart, stuck his chest out, and cleared his throat.

"Mayor Abido speaking, how may I help you?"

"There's a pile of shit in Palm Springs, Mr. Mayor. Check your cell." The line disconnected.

The mayor scurried to his phone and found a text message with a news link of Detective Cravis' alleged murder-suicide with a known felon, Jesse Murdock, who was found with the detective's service weapon.

The mayor threw his phone against the wall, breaking it into multiple pieces.

"Fuuuuuuuuuuuuck!"

TACTICAL

Rain poured in thick sheets with an unrelenting percussion against Detective Rankin's windshield. The wipers swayed rapidly in a futile battle, blurring her view. She turned the knob to the last level, increasing the wipers' speed. Droplets pelted the glass like marbles crashing against the window.

Traffic was light until Rankin turned on the main drag. Brake lights filled the lanes, and drivers moved cautiously to the right lane. She averted the traffic jam and cut through a narrow backstreet and into an alleyway. The single, narrow lane reminded her of a time when she camped out during a stakeout.

The detective's caramel-toned fingers drummed the steering wheel, contemplating her decisions with the mayor, his time bomb of a laptop, Chuck, and Cire. She reminded herself that Cire was just a chess piece on the board. Anything unresolved between them would have to wait or remain unanswered.

Rain splashed Rankin's vehicle in a syncopated manner. She pushed the accelerator and darted from the alley to the street. The gray skies hovered lower over the city as Leticia found her way to the parking lot of Exactly Eggs Diner.

Detective Leticia Rankin stepped out of her car, unfazed by the relentless downpour. The glossy black finish of her double-breasted Michael Kors trench coat shimmered under the pale streetlights, cinched at the waist with a sleek, gold-buckled belt. The coat was tailored to perfection, accentuating her sharp, commanding presence while keeping her completely dry.

Her Anne Klein knee-high leather boots splashed through the puddles with purpose, their four-inch block heels adding height without sacrificing stability.

Her matching wide-brimmed hat sat atop her head, tilted just enough to shield her caramel complexion while letting a few rebellious curls frame her face.

She carried a compact, jet-black umbrella that opened with a smooth, automatic flick—its silver accents catching the glint of passing headlights. As she pushed through the diner's door, shaking the rain from her coat with a graceful sweep, conversations trailed off mid-sentence. Heads turned. Even in the grim haze of a thunderstorm, Detective Rankin commanded the room, her presence magnetic and unshakable.

"Damn," I said, causing Cire to turn to see Leticia, her boots echoing against the tiled floor.

"Rain doesn't wait, and neither do I," she said, lowering into the booth. She asked the server for black coffee with an egg and cheese croissant. Cire and I were fans of the diner's pancakes. Mine had a strawberry topping. Cire asked for a blueberry.

"All right," she said, brushing a stray curl from her forehead. "Time's not on our side, so let's cut to the chase. What's on this thing that has Mayor Abido and the Cyphus Brothers sending people like Detective Cravis and his hitman, Murdock, to Palm Springs – of all places?"

My hands shook a bit. Neither Cire nor I ever looked at the file. JG gave me directions to access the file. I opened the laptop, punched in JG's password, and saw the ominous folder marked **BlackRose**.

"According to Julius," I said, "there's everything from deals, names, locations, and more."

"If half of this is true," Cire chimed in, "it's enough to bring down the mayor—and the Cyphus Brothers—like a house of cards."

Rankin's eyes narrowed. "Let's focus on the Cyphus Brothers first. Take out the muscle, and the mayor will start to squirm."

Cire shifted and moved in close.

"You're sure about this, Leticia? The Cyphus Brothers aren't exactly small-time thugs. They're a well-oiled machine with resources to retaliate—hard."

"I'm counting on it," Rankin replied, her voice steady, almost cold. "The more desperate they get, the more reckless they'll become. And when people like the Cyphus Brothers get reckless, they make mistakes. They're losing money, and money talks."

She leaned forward to focus on the files. The screen's light illuminated her caramel-toned face as the file opened: spreadsheets of money laundering transactions, blurry photos of clandestine meetings, and dossiers on key players—dirty cops, politicians, even judges. Rankin shook her head in disgust.

"This is corruption," she said. "This is a cancer eating through the city."

"Here," she continued, pointing to a file. "A list of shipments coming in through the port. Drugs, arms, contraband—whatever it is, the Cyphus Brothers are running it. We disrupt that pipeline, and we hit them where it hurts. Hard."

I agreed with the detective and suggested utilizing JG more. "He can cross-reference these dates with shipping records. It'll take time, but I'm sure JG might be able to figure out their next big move."

"And you said you two have him somewhere safe, right?"

I smiled, thinking about Gertie. "We've got muscle. too."

Cire folded his arms, watching her with an intensity that hadn't dulled over the years. "And what's the plan when we get that intel? You can't take them down alone, Leticia."

"I'm not asking for permission," she snapped, her gaze meeting his. For a moment, something unspoken passed between them—years of shared history distilled into a heartbeat. I was going to have to keep reminding Cire to let the past be the past. I needed him, but we had shit to handle.

The detective shook her head, focusing back on the screen.

"I'll need you two to keep digging, but be careful. I'm certain everyone's being really cautious now that Cravis' death made headline news."

"Cheese and crackers," Cire said, pulling his phone out from his jacket. "Oh, shit, Bruv, look."

I read the national web news from Cire's phone and looked up to see Leticia looking right at me.

"Find any weak links in their operation—people who might flip under pressure. The Cyphus Brothers have built their empire on loyalty bought with fear. We break that, and the rest will crumble."

"And the mayor?" I asked.

Rankin smiled—a sharp, dangerous curve of her lips. "He's smart, but he's soft. Once the Cyphus Brothers start falling apart, he'll panic. When he does, we'll be ready, because he's throwing someone under the bus."

"Let's move," she said, snapping the laptop shut.

"I'll text you both with a number to use. For now, this is the best plan we have. The Cyphus Brothers are already on Metro's radar, so if I ask for a couple of favors, they'll think I'm chasing the case."

She slid out of the booth first, put on her raincoat, and then her hat. She looked at Cire and me with a cautioning gaze and walked out of the diner into the storm. Cire exchanged a look with Leticia and returned to his blueberry pancakes. He knew full well the storm we were about to embark on with the Cyphus Brothers was going to be as fierce as the raging storm outside.

THE GILDED CAGE

The soft hum of lo-fi hip-hop and jazz infused through The Gilded Cage, blending with murmurs, whispers, keen moans, and occasional clinks of champagne flutes.

Quentin Cyphus leaned against the bar with effortless charm, his Hugo Boss suit impeccably tailored, every inch of him exuding confidence. The dim lighting played against his Greek features, enhancing the roguish grin he flashed at the bartender, who seemed both flattered and wary under his gaze. There was something magnetic about him—a force of personality that could draw people in before they realized they might regret it. He took his drink and joined his brother.

Corey, on the other hand, sat in the shadows of their private booth, his reserved demeanor a stark contrast to his younger brother's flamboyance. The elder Cyphus carried an air of quiet calculation, his sharp eyes scanning the room like a predator observing its prey. Every movement was deliberate, every word measured. Even the double-breasted blazer he wore was intentionally planned.

Mayor Jefferson Abido entered with his usual companion from his office trysts. This evening, however, she wore an emerald dress with asymmetrical wraps around her fit body. Her arms were defined and toned. She draped the mayor's arm casually as they walked through Gertie and Sarya's club.

Appearing relaxed, Jefferson's mind roiled beneath his politician's mask. None of the recent activities – Cravis' death, Julius on the loose with his laptop, and Murdock's failure – boded in his favor for re-election or his fragile alliance with the Cyphus Brothers.

In the corner booth, Corey and Quentin Cyphus watched the mayor and his companion approach. Corey, the eldest, remained seated, his demeanor cold and deliberate. Quentin, ever the charmer, rose with a grin that could disarm anyone - even the suspicious.

"Mr. Mayor," Quentin greeted, extending his hand. "What a pleasure it is to see you tonight. And your charming companion, of course. What a dress."

Jefferson managed a tight smile, shaking Quentin's hand before slipping into the booth. He reached across the table to Corey, but his piercing gaze suggested otherwise. His stare cut through Jefferson like a scalpel. Jefferson's companion excused herself, leaving the men to their discussion.

"Cravis is dead," Corey began. "Murdock, also dead. This is a problem."

His voice steady and low, Jefferson said, "I know. It's not…well, it's unfortunate."

"Unfortunate?" Quentin leaned forward, the smile slipping from his face. "Murdock was supposed to recover that laptop. Cravis was supposed to ensure there were no loose ends. Instead, he created a mess with the elderly couple and created a bigger stir."

"Now both of them are gone," Quentin continued, "and that Julius guy is still out there with your fuckin' laptop. This isn't unfortunate, Jefferson. This is a fucking calamity."

A server wearing a resemblance to a Playboy Bunny costume brought the gentlemen their usual drinks. Jefferson grabbed his sniffer and consumed it in one gulp. He gasped and told the waitress to come back with the bottle.

"Do you think I don't understand the stakes here?" Jefferson said, clearing his throat from the bourbon. "Cravis' death complicates things, but I'm working on containing the fallout."

"Contain it with the quickness," Corey said with ice in his tone. "The longer that laptop is unaccounted for, the more exposure we all have – including your brother."

Jefferson's chest tightened at the mention of Charleston. His younger brother's mistakes had dragged him into this quagmire, and now his political career could be snipped like a loose thread on a sweater.

"No one knows about Charlie's involvement."

"For now," Quentin responded. "Secrets remain secrets for only so long, Mr. Mayor. Bodies are piling up from our city all the way to Palm fuckin' Springs. El Cucuy was in our fucking city, for crissakes!"

Corey grunted, pointing at the mayor, "If someone connects Cravis, Murdock, and that laptop, it's only a matter of time before they find Charleston, you, and us."

Jefferson sat back. His mind was racing and spiraling in hate. He hated the Cyphus Brothers. He hated their control over him. He hated that this would impact his campaign if he were exposed, and he hated that Charleston was mixed up in all of this, but he needed to keep the brothers calm and supportive; otherwise, Charleston would already be dead.

"What do you suggest we do?" Jefferson said, forcing his winning, mayoral smile.

Quentin stood searching for someone. He smiled at the sight of a beautiful redhead in a cream, see-through, crew neck fitted dress approaching. His grin returned.

"Find Julius and make sure the laptop never sees the light of day."

"In the meantime, Mr. Mayor," Corey added, "you keep doing what you do best. Smile for the cameras, shake hands, kiss babies, and keep this city running. The last thing we need is you falling apart."

Jefferson nodded. Quentin and Corey rose as their respective dates returned to join them. They had keys to their private rooms. Jefferson's companion returned to his side as well with a warm smile. She tongued his ear and grabbed his thigh. He closed his eyes, attempting to regain control. His companion held up a key to their private room. She extended her hand. Jefferson smiled, although he felt like the walls were closing in.

DIRTY GERTIE & SARYA- THE DUO

The Gilded Cage, where opulence masked intrigue, Dirty Gertie paced the secluded back room, her polished boots clicking against the marble floor. Her red, floral kimono swayed with each step.

The surveillance feeds from the club played across several monitors on the wall, each screen offering a different angle of the lounge. To the untrained eye, it might have looked like overzealous security, but for Gertie and Sarya, it was an intricate web of control—one they had honed through years of training in the world's most clandestine organizations.

Gertie stood behind the bar, her sharp eyes scanning the room like a hawk surveying prey. Her heavy bangles clicked against the bar as she set a glass down in front of a patron, a practiced smile masking the calculations behind her gaze. At one of the private booths, Mayor Abido sat stiffly with the Cyphus Brothers. Their body language screamed tension, even as they kept their voices hushed.

"Sarya," Gertie muttered, her voice low enough to blend with the jazz filtering through the club. Sarya appeared from the shadows, her movements fluid, her dark eyes gleaming with curiosity. "Booth nine. Mayor and those Cyphus madaphuqs. The mics picking up anything?"

Sarya pulled a tablet from her bag and tapped a few commands. The screen lit up with an audio feed, faint and crackling but discernible.

The mayor's voice carried through, tight with frustration. *"Cravis is dead. So is your hitman. This is spiraling out of control."*

"Sounds like things are heating up," Sarya said, her lips curving into a wry smile.

Gertie nodded; her expression unreadable. "They're planning something, but they're running scared. That's good for us." She tapped the bar, her mind already spinning with possibilities. "Chuck and Cire need to hear this."

"Mayor's looking twitchy," Sarya remarked, perched on the edge of a sleek desk as she watched the Cyphus Brothers exchange hushed words with Abido. "Makes you wonder how long he can hold it together."

Gertie snorted, adjusting the volume on one of the feeds. "Not long. That madaphuq got that 'cornered rat' look. And the brothers got him under their thumb. All we need to do is apply the right amount of pressure."

The pair worked with seamless precision, their movements a silent testament to their training. Recruited years ago by the CIA, then cycling through the ranks of other three-letter agencies, Gertie and Sarya had seen it all—espionage, covert operations, the delicate art of dismantling empires without ever setting foot in a courthouse. The Gilded Cage was their latest stage, and they played their parts to perfection as sex club hostesses.

Sarya tapped a few keys on her laptop, isolating the audio feed from the mayor's booth. The heated argument between Abido and the Cyphus Brothers filled the room.

"...make sure no one connects the dots," Abido's voice hissed, barely masking his desperation. *"We find Julius. No loose ends."*

Sarya glanced at Gertie. "Want me to clean it up and send it to Chuck?"

"Not just yet," Gertie replied, leaning against the desk and crossing her arms. "This is bigger than Julius. If we're gonna help Chuck and Cire, they need the full picture. Not just the mayor's panic attack."

Sarya smirked; her sharp features illuminated by the glow of the screens. "What's the play, then?"

Gertie's eyes narrowed as she watched the Cyphus Brothers rise from their seats, their expressions cold and calculating. "We dig deeper. If the Cyphus madaphuqs are this agitated, it's not just the laptop they're worried about. There's more to this puzzle, and I want every piece before we make a move on these bloodclots."

Sliding the tablet back into her bag, Sarya nodded. "I'll drive out to Chuck's with the audio file. He needs to hear exactly what's going down."

Gertie smirked, leaning forward on the bar. "And tell him this isn't a favor. It's a partnership. They came to us, so if they take the Cyphus Brothers down, it's good for everyone. You be mindful, he's married, and we saved his wife and daughter."

"Girl, please. I ain't worried 'bout Chuck as much as he ain't thinking about me. We were frickin teens, kids practically."

"So you say, gyal," Gertie said. "Been seeing how you two are sneaking peeks at each other."

"I can look."

"Don't touch."

DETECTION

The trio was back at the Exactly Egg diner in a larger booth. Leticia tipped the waitress handsomely for non-stop cups of coffee and for keeping the neighboring booths empty.

I scrolled through a list of shipping records, muttering to myself, while Cire sat with his arms crossed, quietly observing Rankin with that same unreadable intensity.

Then, amidst the names and dossiers on the laptop, a familiar one appeared—*Charleston Abido*. The color drained slightly from my face.

"Uh… Rankin? You need to see this."

Rankin glanced up sharply, her lips tightening as I turned the laptop toward her. The file labeled **Charleston** opened with a single click, revealing a series of financial documents and incriminating messages. Rankin's eyes darted over the contents, her frown deepening.

"Charleston Abido," she murmured. "The mayor's younger brother. Of course."

"Do you know him?" Cire asked, leaning forward.

Rankin gave a curt nod. "Not personally, but his name's come up before—petty crimes, gambling debts. Never anything that stuck."

She straightened; her voice edged with frustration. "But this? This is a whole new level. It looks like Charleston skimmed money off the Cyphus Brothers' operations, and when they found out, he dragged his brother—the *mayor*—into this mess to save his own skin."

I let out a low whistle.

"So, the mayor's been helping the Cyphus Brothers to keep Charleston alive?"

"Looks that way," Rankin said grimly. "Charleston played a dangerous game, and now he's in too deep. The Cyphus Brothers probably see him as a liability. If we lean on him, he might fold to protect his brother—or himself."

Cire raised an eyebrow. "And you think we can trust anything he says?"

"No," Rankin replied flatly, her caramel-toned features hardening. "But we don't need to trust him. We just need to put enough pressure on him to break the Cyphus Brothers' hold."

We sat in the booth, a tense silence falling over us as we exchanged glances. Finally, Cire broke. "What's the play, Leticia?"

"We reach out to Charleston, quietly," she said, her voice steady with resolve. "If the Cyphus Brothers think we're onto him, they'll cut him loose—or worse. We make him believe that cooperating with us is the only way to save himself and his brother."

"And when he breaks?" I asked hesitantly.

Rankin's gaze sharpened, her tone like a blade's edge. "When he breaks, we use what he gives us to take the Cyphus Brothers down. Once they're out of the way, Mayor Abido will have nowhere left to hide."

The laptop hummed softly, its damning contents glowing like an unholy altar. Rankin leaned back, her mind already racing ahead. Charleston Abido might not be trustworthy, but he was a crack in the foundation. And Rankin was more than ready to turn that crack into a collapse.

UNCOVERING

Rain continued the next day. Cire rested on my chaise lounge, and I couldn't believe he was snoring. We'd been non-stop since Palm Springs and needed a break. I felt invigorated with new energy since I returned home and to my bed. The only thing missing was my wife and daughter. Luckily, they were safe.

The house was eerily quiet, even with Cire's breathing. I didn't feel like watching sports, news, or anything on TV. I continued to study the files and the names, and printed out anything from the laptop that seemed like a bigger puzzle piece.

The tap on my front door woke Cire. He reached for his 9mm, but I waved him off. Even with all the drama, a knock on the door meant just the opposite. Sarya stepped in, shaking off droplets of rain from her leather jacket.

"Gerties is keeping the lights low at the Cage," Sarya said. She placed a small recorder on the table as Cire approached, still half asleep.

"Wagwan, Rah?"

"Hey, C. I've got something good," Sarya said, pointing at the recorder.

My eyes widened, "The mayor?"

"And the Cyphus Brothers," Sarya confirmed, tapping the recorder. "They're shook. Murdock and Cravis' deaths are creating chaos, and they've pinned everything on getting Julius and the laptop. The entire recording is right here -- it's bad, Chuck. Bad but good."

Cire picked up the recorder. "So, what's the dilly? What are we searching for?"

"Jefferson Abido – the mayor and the mayor of this mess – is on here barely holding it together," Sarya said.

"Corey Cyphus keeps everything, including the mayor, on a tight leash. Quentin is a walking, ticking time bomb with a smile. He's volatile, and Jefferson is stuck between trying to appease them and keeping his re-election hopes alive."

Cire and I exchanged assured glances. "We've got something too, Rah," Cire said. He nodded to me with a 'you tell her' look.

"Julius found financial records tied directly to Charleston Abido. It shows Charleston siphoned off money from the Cyphus Brothers and used his brother, the mayor, to cover his tracks. This connects the dots between the brothers and Jefferson."

Sarya placed her hands on her hips. "The Abidos are compromised figures. So, what's up? Whatcha tryna do?"

Cire leaned forward, "According to all the crap in these files, the Cyphus Brothers are expecting a shipment soon—contraband through the port. If we intercept it, we hit them where it hurts. We need Charleston to turn on them."

"And how do you plan to do that?" Sarya asked, raising an eyebrow. "Charleston's more likely to flee than fight."

"Charleston messed up, but deep down, he's trying to protect his brother," I said. "If we can convince him to flip, we tell him it's the only way to save Jefferson, and we might have a shot."

Sarya's sharp gaze shifted between Cire and me, measuring our tenacity. "It's risky. The Cyphus Brothers are pros. They've got heat, and with a snap of a finger, their Greek army would swoop down."

"Then we make sure they never see us coming," Cire said firmly. He gestured to the laptop. "This is all we've got to work with, Bruv. Between Julius's files and your recording, we've got enough to tie the Abidos to the Cyphus Brothers. We can blow the lid off their entire operation."

Sarya smirked, sliding the recorder toward me. "You're going to need a damn good team to pull this off."

"Good thing we've got you and Gertie. Though Cire clipped El Cucuy at Robbie's wedding, I was waiting to see what the sista soldiers were going to do."

"Oh, y'all didn't want that smoke," she said, grabbing her jacket. "I'll loop Gertie in. In the meantime, you figure out how to get Charleston to talk."

"I'm on it."

Sarya pointed at her wrist, "Time's ticking."

As Sarya slipped out into the rain, Cire and I knew it was time to get down with the get down.

"We gotta tell Leticia, Bruv," Cire said.

Placing my hand on Cire's shoulder, I told him, "You handle that, my guy."

STEPS

Detective Rankin sat in her car, the rhythmic tapping of rain against the windshield blending with the low hum of the engine. She watched two people dash to the bus stop for shelter. Cire's name flashed across her phone screen, and for a moment, she hesitated. Then, with a resigned sigh, she answered.

"Cire," she said curtly. "What's up?"

"Leticia," his voice came through steady, but with concern, maybe. "We've got something. Sarya recorded the mayor and the Cyphus Brothers at the Gilded Cage. You need to hear it."

Rubbing her temple, then her forehead, she asked, "You've got a recording from a private, exclusive adult club? Do you have any idea what kind of firestorm this could start if it gets out?"

"I get it," Cire said quickly. "But you need to listen to it before you dismiss it. The Cyphus Brothers are threatening the mayor, and they're putting everything on getting that laptop back. This is big, Leticia."

"And this recording," she pressed, her voice sharp. "How exactly did Sarya manage to get it? That place isn't exactly a public square."

"Gertie and Sarya aren't just club owners," Cire replied, his tone steady but serious. "They're former black ops, Leticia. Langley, Virginia, kind of ops. They've got skills, resources, and connections. They're in this to take down people like the Cyphus Brothers."

Leticia's grip on the phone tightened. "And who do they work for?"

"I don't know," Cire admitted. "But I trust them. And if you let them, they'll be the nail in the Cyphus Brothers' coffin."

She didn't speak. She stared out at the rain-slicked street, her thoughts racing. "Cire," she said with doubt. "If this blows up, this could be my job. My career. You realize that, don't you?"

"I do."

"So, what are we doing? This is a real risk, Cire."

"I know you're a bad-mamma-jamma, but we can't take them down alone. You told us yourself you didn't know who you could trust inside Metro. We need Gertie and Sarya. They can help with Charleston."

Leticia's chest tightened at the mention of Charleston. "Jefferson's dirty," she said. "But he's doing all of this to protect his brother. I can't ignore the fact that Charleston started all of this and doesn't want to die, and Jefferson is, well, he doesn't want to lose his brother."

"Maybe Jefferson's not a lost cause. But he's made his choices, Leticia. He's in too deep now. We both know there's no saving him without taking down the Cyphus Brothers."

The detective closed her eyes, letting his words sink in. She drummed the steering wheel.

"You still there, Leticia?"

"Send me the recording," she said after a long silence. "I'll listen. But Cire, we have to move carefully, okay? I don't want to clean up another mess."

"You know me, Leticia. Careful is not really my style, Luv."

A faint smile tugged at the corner of her lips. "Yeah, well, just don't do anything stupid."

As the call ended, Leticia sat for a moment longer, staring at her phone. Their past was still a cold case between them, unresolved but not forgotten. With all her doubts, a small part of her was glad Cire called.

THE ARRANGEMENT

Charleston Abido stepped into the dimly lit lounge of a boutique hotel; his nerves barely masked by his polished exterior. He wore a stylish Edward Fraiser blazer and checkered slacks. He adjusted his tie, gazing around the room until it landed on Gertie. She was seated at the bar, her curvy figure draped in a sleek black Futario dress that hugged her in all the right places. Her presence was magnetic, commanding attention without effort.

Charleston hesitated for a moment before approaching her. He drew closer, and recognition flickered. His eyes widened. "You," his voice low. "I've seen you at the Gilded Cage."

Gertie turned to him, her lips curving into a knowing smile. "If you've seen me there, then you know what time it is."

Charleston's throat tightened, but he managed to smile and nod. "No doubt. Whatcha wanna do?"

Standing and gesturing toward the exit, Gertie said, "I want to talk, but somewhere private."

"Talk, huh? That's what we're calling it these days? Cool, let's go talk."

Charleston followed her out, his mind racing, but excited. I pulled up in a black Tahoe wearing the typical chauffeur's get-up. We drove less than three city blocks and arrived at the W Hotel. Charleston tried to make a move on Gertie in the backseat, but she held up her hand and pointed at me.

"We'll have some privacy in minutes."

Charleston shook his head in agreement. His nerves were frayed, but he maintained his composure. Gertie led him to the penthouse suite, her poise undaunted. When the door opened, Charleston froze, his gaze sweeping over the room and landing on the group waiting for him.

Charleston's eyes narrowed. "What, what the fuck is this?" He turned to leave, but I was standing at the door, motioning for him to come inside.

Leticia stepped into the light, flashing her badge. "This, you ask? This is your opportunity to make things right. Sit down."

The penthouse suite at the W Hotel was a picture of understated luxury, its floor-to-ceiling windows offering a glittering view of the city skyline. Charleston was outnumbered. Cire paced near the bar, his movements restless, while Sarya leaned against the wall, her arms crossed, her sharp eyes zoned in on Charleston. The city lights framed Gertie's silhouette, her face scrawled.

The younger Abido's nervous energy filled the room as he reluctantly took a seat. His eyes shifted to me, then Cire, and over to Sarya.

"I've seen you at the Cage too," Charleston said, pointing at Sarya. She sniffed and walked into the living room area. "What the fuck is going on? You can't bust me for fucking."

Cire broke the silence. "That's not why you're here, Bruv."

Charleston scoffed, but it lacked conviction. "Then, what's up? This ain't legit if you're trapping me up here with a cop. You must think I have something you need."

I leaned forward, arms behind my back. "Not think. Know. Charleston, we've got files linking you to the Cyphus Brothers. "Financial records, deals—everything. You're in deeper than you want to be, and if they find out you're even *talking* to us, you're done."

Charleston shifted in his seat. "You think I don't know that? You think I don't know how dangerous those two are? I've seen what they're capable of, so fuck those records or files. My brother is protecting me."

Leticia stood next to me, her voice steady and sharp. "They're powerful. But that power is built on fear. Fear of exposure, fear of losing control. And that's exactly what we can give them—a reason to be afraid."

Charleston's gaze snapped to her; his lips pressed into a thin line. "Do you know, I mean, actually know what you're asking me to do? And what do I get out of this? A pat on the back? You have no idea what I've been through to stay alive."

"No, I don't," Leticia admitted, her tone softening just enough to catch him off guard. "But I know you don't want to keep living like this—under their thumb, looking over your shoulder, waiting for the day they decide you're no longer worth the effort. That's no way to live."

Charleston slumped in his chair, running a hand over his face. He shook his head, staring at his shoes.

"Corey," he started, "he's cold, calculated. He's like the boss of the bosses. He snaps his finger, and it's lights out. Quentin? He'll strike without warning if he thinks you're a threat. If I do this—if I flip—it's not just me they'll come for. It will be Jefferson, too. Hell, they'll come after my entire family."

"Then let's make sure they don't have the chance," Sarya cut in from the living room, her voice crisp and decisive. "We have a plan to intercept their next shipment. If we take out their pipeline, their grip on this city starts to loosen. But to do that, we need you, Charleston."

"You're their weak link, you madaphuq" Gertie snapped, stepping forward. "And that's not a bad thing, ya know. Call it an opportunity. You give us what we need to take them down, and we make sure they can't touch you, your brother, everyone."

Charleston's hands clenched into fists, his mind racing. He looked up at the detective.

"How can I trust you? How do I know you won't just hang me out to dry or throw me in jail once you get what you want?"

Leticia held his gaze, contemplating her words carefully. She knew this was all or nothing.

"Charleston, I'm one of the good cops in this city. Not the rat bastards Corey and Quentin have on their payroll, not to mention anyone your brother has brought in to protect him."

Charleston stood, "That's not fair. That's not what happened. The city manager and one of the councilwomen got wrapped up in some drug shit with Quentin."

We all waited for Charleston to finish.

"Councilwoman Harris copped some Tramadol for her son. He's this big-time athlete with a bunch of D1 offers and he fucked up his knee. The city manager introduced the councilwoman to Quentin because he had done the same thing for his daughter. You know, the one who got the gold medal in the Olympics? Well,

Quentin gave her a nice batch at the Cage for some action. She's a freaky bitch."

Cire sucked his teeth. "Blood clot. Scandal everywhere, Bruv. Finish, man. Keep going."

"Quentin found an in with the city manager. He threatened to expose everyone unless he could get protection with the shipments. He got Gene Cravis involved, and Cravis pulled in his guys. If something got too out of control, Cravis would send one of his goons on payroll. Murdock was one of them. There was a lot of cash flowing," Charleston said with a greedy grimace.

"There was no way. They knew I was skimming, but they had checks and balances in place on top of their own checks and balances. Once I got hemmed up, they pulled Jefferson in on it. The first place they took him to negotiate was the Gilded Cage. Threw a lot of pussy at him, taped it and, boom, he's caught in the matrix."

The room fell silent. Expression unwavering, Leticia paced the room. Sarya mumbled, 'wow' as she recalled Charleston's rant. Gertie and Cire studied Charleston, searching for a hole in the story. I leaned against the dining room table.

"Well," Leticia said. "You've seen what they can do. It's time to end it. I don't know if I can protect you or your brother, but it's clear he's involved to protect you."

The room fell into another tense silence, every eye on Charleston as he wrestled with the decision before him. Finally, he exhaled, his shoulders slumping in defeat. "Fine, fuck it," he said quietly. "I'll help you. But if this goes south…"

"It won't," Cire and I said in unison.

DISMANTLE

For the next three days, we planned the biggest operation of our lives. Charleston told us where we could post up at the docks without being noticed or getting shot. Cire said he'd find a place and clip anything that moved, including the Cyphus brothers. I reminded him that Leticia didn't give us clearance to kill the head of the snake, but Cire said it wouldn't matter if it got hot. I didn't disagree.

The salty breeze carried the reek of rust and oil. The docks were shrouded in darkness as I crouched behind a shipping container with my favorite pistol. Nervousness overwhelmed me as my grip increased when I heard movement. Detective Leticia Rankin was moving into position with one of her guys. They both wore Kevlar vests around their tactical gear and boots. Leticia had more clips, holsters, and weapons than Batman's utility belt.

"Phillips, Chuck, Chuck, Phillips," Leticia said, introducing me to her partner. "Phillips knows the deal, and he's a mean son-of-a-bitch with that MP5. If shit goes sideways, he's on the ready."

We gave each other a nod and connected our headsets for communication. Phillips fumbled with his night vision goggles and placed them on his helmet. Leticia did a radio check with everyone. Cire did not respond.

"Cire! Do you copy?"

I tapped the detective on the shoulder and shook my head. "Don't worry about C. He's locked in."

"But what if..."

"Nope," I interjected. "No 'ifs,' C is out there, ready to go."

The Cyphus Brothers' last major shipment arrived – weapons, narcotics, and enough firepower to fund their empire for years. Anything that was listed under the **Black Rose** file was likely coming off that vessel.

Corey and Quentin Cyphus arrived in a Black-on-black Chevy Tahoe. A few of their men approached the SUV for instructions. They were draped with an assortment of AR-15s and other weapons.

Sarya and Gertie moved like shadows between crates. Jevaun ducked behind the container next to Phillips. He pulled a flask from his vest and took a swig.

"Drinking on the job, J?"

"Whatever, man, this is my personal fusion of ashwagandha powder and kiwi strawberry electrolytes. Keeps me light on my feet and hyped."

"Copy."

Quentin paced by the dock's edge, barking orders to the grunts unloading crates from the cargo ship *Libra Night*. Dozens of smugglers worked under the dim, yellow lights, stacking boxes and checking inventory. Corey leaned against the Tahoe and lit a cigar. We could smell the strong, aromatic Cohiba from where we crouched.

Two trucks were guided off the ship, which got Leticia's attention. "Don't tell me these fuckers are trafficking people too."

"We're stopping all that bullshit tonight," Sarya responded.

Leticia made the call, "If everyone's in position, let's move in. Backup is waiting for my signal."

I went first, Jevaun followed me, flanking me to my side. Leticia and Phillips skirted to the left of the shipment containers to get close to the SUV.

Then— Click. Clack. Clink. Scrape.

Phillip's night vision goggles slipped off his helmet, drawing attention to the darkness. One of the guards heard it as his head snapped in our direction.

"The fuck was that?" he muttered, reaching for his pistol. As his first step crunched the gravel beneath him, he didn't make a second.

Cire took the shot.

The guard's head snapped back in a spray of blood before he could shout a warning. His body slumped against a container.

Gunfire erupted. Phillips and Rankin surged from cover, taking out the nearest guards. Jevaun opened fire from the flanks, driving the crew in a chaotic scramble. Two shots whizzed by me, and I returned fire. I heard a thud and a grunt but kept moving. From above, Cire began to work his magic with lethal precision.

Zip! Man down.

Zup-Zup! Another with his chest cavity caved in.

Zip! A skull punctured, body crumpling lifeless against a stack of crates.

Cire ended eight of Cyphus' men with a whispering bullet to the brain each time they attempted to close in on us.

Sarya and Gertie worked in deadly synchronization, slicing through the confronting brutes. One of Cyphus' men charged in my direction, pointing an AK-47 at me. Before he could fire, Sarya was behind him, her blade slipping between his ribs. He gurgled, hands twitching, and she let him slide off her knife with his dead weight.

I smiled like a proud parent and saluted her. "Still got those skills, huh?"

"They never left, Chucky!"

Another man lunged at Gertie with a crowbar. She ducked, spun, and buried her combat blade into his gut. He gasped, choking, and she twisted the handle, watching the life drain from his eyes. She gave him a kick to the torso and yelled, "Razor sharp and very lethal, you madaphuq!"

As Phillips approached the older Cyphus, he turned and shot the cop. He went down but wasn't dead as the ceramic-plated protected him. Corey ran for the SUV.

Rankin unloaded her clip, shooting everyone around the Cyphus man except Cyphus. "Somebody stopped that bastard!" she yelled.

"I got him," Cire muttered from the rooftop.

He adjusted his aim, exhaled, and squeezed the trigger. Corey's knee exploded. Collapsing against the SUV, his scream echoed through the dock area. Blood spurted from the shot, pooling on the pavement. He wasn't going anywhere as his piercing cries increased in intensity. Rankin handcuffed him to the vehicle.

"It's over, Cyphus," Rankin said. "Sit tight."

Quentin recognized his brother's cries and ran toward us, firing blindly with a sawed-off shotgun.

Gertie sidestepped the blast like Neo averting bullets in The Matrix. She sidestepped by a barrel and launched her knife like a throwing star. The blade spun end over end before burying into the back of Quentin's neck. He staggered almost ten feet, making a wet, gurgling noise. He dropped the shotgun to reach for the blade, but to no avail. Quentin caromed off the crates, knocking them over, and Sarya was on him before he could fall.

She ripped the knife free from Quentin's hand as he yelped in anguish. Sarya shoved the knife deep into his chest for good measure and watched the light fade from his eyes. "That for the girls, your traffic, you punk ass bitch!"

Quentin collapsed, twitching and twisting for life, but fell still.

SPLASH

Cire chimed in our earpieces, "He's cooked with curry."

The docks fell quiet except for the lapping waves and the distant wail of sirens. Rankin holstered her weapon, surveying the area and the carnage.

"ATF and DEA are en route," Leticia said. "I purposely delayed the intel so we could handle this, but they'll be heading to the mayor's mansion too."

She looked at the makeshift team.

"I'll make the statements, and if it's alright with you, Chuck, I'll keep the ladies with me – all things considered."

"I get it," I responded. "They're still, how do I say, connected with Langley."

"You two cool with that?" Leticia asked, turning to Sarya and Gertie.

Gertie twirled her blade before sliding it into its sheath. "Always good."

Sarya nodded.

"I'm staying," Jevaun said. "Ain't no way the pros are going to believe three of y'all took out twenty-six men *and* the notorious Cyphus Brothers."

Leticia reached for her holster, "Wanna make it twenty-seven?"

I pulled Jevaun and told him, "Let's make sure we hand over the laptop to the DEA when they arrive at the mayor's place."

Jevaun shook his head in agreement, "Bet. We can do that."

THE APPROACH

The mayor's mansion was a sprawling estate bathed in soft golden lights from the entryway leading up to his door. Manicured hedges, bushes, and marble pillars screamed wealth and power. Based on what I learned in the past few months, these now parallel the similarities of corruption.

I imagined Mayor Jefferson Abido and his brother Charleston sipping whiskey, laughing at the recent events at the docks, and believing themselves untouchable. I had mixed feelings like Leticia for a moment. Perhaps the mayor was covering his tracks with his meticulous, methodical, maniacal people log. Perhaps he thought that keeping records of who was corrupt, who was engaging in shady dealings with the Cyphus brothers, and who was being dealt with would protect him and his brother. Yet, through resiliency, his brother started this shitstorm, and Julius Givens, the moonlighting techie, poured high-octane gasoline on everything.

I had the mayor's laptop gripped to my side. We have already transferred the evidence to multiple hard drives and a remote server. Still, I wanted him to see the device that housed all the evidence of drug and human trafficking, money laundering, weapons, and additional dirty secrets of his fellow councilmembers. The recordings from the Cage would be thrown out in court, but no one knew that at the time.

Cire and Jevaun approached the wrought-iron gates with me. Cire scanned the area. "We got guards posted at the entrance, probably armed. Do attempt a subtle approach?"

"I ain't in no mood for subtle," Jevaun said.

"J's right," I said. "Leticia informed us to get in before the DEA showed up, so let's make it happen."

"Do your thing, Bruv," Cire stated. "Imma find a way to keep you covered."

Jevaun and I approached the gate, and to my surprise, the men appeared stylish in black, tailored suits. They both possessed fit, athletic physiques, and I wondered if they were Corey and Quentin's men. Clearly, the mayor could afford security without requesting a detail from the Cyphus brothers, but I wasn't so sure. These men were composed and alert.

"No visitors," the guard said, hand hovering over his holster.

I held up the laptop, and Jevaun held his hands up in a lighthearted way.

"Mayor Abido is expecting this."

"Not at this hour, so I recommend you two gentlemen be on your way."

"Why does it always have to be us?" Jevaun asked, looking at me. "How come we can't get along? Isn't that what Rodney the king said? We Black, you're Black, the mayor's Black, and it seems we can never get our shit together and be on the up-and-up."

The second guard unclipped his holster. "Sir, I'm telling you, turn around and leave the premises before we have to use force."

Cire's suppressed rifle whispered from the darkness. The guard creased backward to the pavement. Before the second guard moved, Jevaun drove his fist into his throat, then caught him as he choked him between the gates. He struggled for roughly thirteen seconds before he went limp.

"I was hoping one of them would walk up on us," Jevaun said. "I got the remote."

Jevaun pressed the button, and the mansion gates opened. I suggested cutting through the garden just in case more men were patrolling the grounds. Cire said he had us covered, and I believed him.

We decided to enter through the front. The grand doors were unlocked. I imagined the good mayor would not expect trouble to walk through his front door. We stepped inside, and the air smelled of expensive cigars and the scent of illicit wealth. Soulful music played in the study. D'Angelo's *Send It On* echoed in the hallway. In a muffled yet distinct way, jovial laughter and joyous camaraderie were transpiring behind the doors.

"They have company," Jevaun observed. "Ready to ruin their night?"

I smirked. "Born ready."

Jevaun pushed open the study doors. Three women were adorned in Savage X Fenty lingerie and Christian Louboutin heels. One woman wore a sheer, see-through top and the mayor's blazer. She was sitting on the mayor's lap behind his mahogany desk. Another woman had on velvet pajamas exposing her breasts, and the third woman draped herself in rubies, sapphires, and pearls over her corset. I only saw the front part of her thong. The string in the back took refuge between her BBL. She was standing next to Charleston, who had a glass of bourbon in his hand. Everyone froze.

"Well, well," the mayor said, smoothly swirling his drink. "These must be the gentleman you told me about, Charleston."

The mayor's brother sniffed. "Yeah, that's them."

"And look. They returned my laptop. Please give Julius my regards. You are the one responsible for keeping him alive, right?"

Jevaun and I didn't respond.

"Look, man, I didn't want him snuffed out," the mayor said, "I just wanted to retrieve what was rightfully mine. Had we had conversed about what he saw, what he found, you know, said files; he would have been paid handsomely to keep his mouth shut."

The mayor stood, kissed his mate with a light smooch, and walked towards me.

"But, nooooo. He decided to run off to Palm Springs and delay progress."

"Say, man, did you know the Cyphus brothers were running girls?" Jevaun asked.

"My only obligation to the Cyphus brothers was to ensure they would not be implicated for doing business in my city, thanks to my brother."

I stepped in front of the mayor. "The Cyphus brothers used you to cover their criminal empire because of your brother, and you could've stopped it. Instead, you used that energy and built another layer. Your brother didn't have anything to do with Cravis or Murdock in Palm Springs."

Charleston stepped towards me, and Jevaun blocked his path. The mayor walked back to his desk and beckoned his date. They leaned back in his chair and sipped more bourbon.

"This was a mistake, gentlemen. One big mistake."

I leaned on his desk, pointing, "No, Mayor. The mistake is you sitting there thinking you're untouchable."

The mayor laughed. Taking another sip, he set his glass down. "Do you really think walking in here with my laptop gives you the power…. are you thinking you're that guy? You have no idea how deep this goes."

Charleston reached behind his back.

Cire's voice crackled in my earpiece.

"He's got heat, Chuck."

I moved first and fast, drawing my pistol and aiming it between Charleston's eyes. The ladies shrieked and moved to the other side of the room.

"Try it," I said.

Charleston froze and raised his hands.

"Mr. Mayor, call your lawyer and get one for your brother, too."

The mayor shook his head and exhaled. He took another sip of his bourbon. "You still don't get it. I am the people's mayor. I'm up for re-election. I don't go to prison. I won't go to prison."

I heard the sirens and saw the red and blue lights flashing through the windows. That was my queue.

"Tonight's your night to find out, Mr. Mayor," I said.

Jevaun pointed at the women. "I suggest y'all put some clothes on before the men in the blue jackets walk up in here."

ACCOMPLISHED

The dust barely settled at the docks and the mansion when the reality of our triumph sank in. The Cyphus Brothers' operation was dismantled, the mayor and his brother were in custody, and my crew made it out without a scratch on their forehead.

We leaned against a patrol car waiting for Leticia to arrive at the mayor's mansion. A white Ford Expedition pulled up to the gate. The mayor's party guests were excused and entered the SUV. The back passenger side window slid down. "Thank you, sir," said a twisted loc-haired woman.

I shook my head and pulled out my phone. It rang twice.

"Chuck? Is everything okay?"

I smiled, the tension easing from my shoulders, hearing my wife's voice.

"It's over, Alana. You and Sara can come home now."

I heard a deep breath, a moment of silence, and a relieved sob. "Thank God. Thank you, Jesus. We've been so worried, Chuck, especially after all the stuff in Palm Springs."

"I know, darling," I said softly. "But it's done. Everyone's safe. I'll see you when you get home. Tell Sara I love her."

I hung up and texted JG: *All is well. The mayor is in handcuffs. Great work.*

Leticia shook hands with some DEA honchos. One of them patted her on the shoulder. She looked relaxed and relieved as she approached me. I was still looking at my phone.

"Everything okay?" she asked.

"Yeah, Alana, my wife, and my daughter, Sara, are coming home. They took some time away while we, uh, sorted all this out."

Leticia laughed and placed her hand on my shoulder. "You did well, Chuck. Let's get together for a drink. It'll be my way of saying thanks for bringing this to me."

A tiny smile etched my cheeks. I wanted to tell her it was Cire's idea, but I left it alone.

Code 7 Lounge was a favorite spot for off-duty officers. It was cozy, dimly lit, but the atmosphere was warm and inviting. The bar was filled with conversation and the clinking of glasses, a perfect backdrop for their celebration. Cire let his guard down and joined the team, despite his aversion to cops.

Detective Rankin gave a speech about how honored and humbled she was to work with our team. A few officers and regulars of Code 7 congratulated her and told her she'd be up for commendations for her acts in the line of duty. The local news came on, broadcasting footage of the recent events at the docks and the mayor's mansion. A surge of roars and cheers bellowed throughout the bar when Rankin's face appeared on the screen. Glasses clinked in the air, and a rhythmic pounding on the tables ensued.

"Ran-kin, Ran-kin, Ran-kin, Ran-kin!"

I found Jevaun and Cire shooting pool. Dirty Gertie impressed the officers at the dartboard, and Sarya was chatting with a detective who could have been a body double for Draymond Green.

The bar began to empty. Rankin looked around at us and felt a deep sense of pride and connection. I'm sure she has never felt this way within her own department. Most of them were on the mayor's payroll. I saw her walk outside, imagining she needed a moment to herself.

"Mind if I join you?" Cire's voice was hesitant.

Rankin turned and smiled. "Not at all. I could use the company."

Cire leaned against the railing beside her. The unspoken words, the silence between them, filled the night air.

"We did it," Leticia said, breaking the silence.

"It was pretty intense and peak."

"You haven't lost your skills. You should consider …"

Cire sucked his teeth, "Don't even."

Rankin laughed and turned to Cire. "Look, C, I know things ended utterly bizarre between us a while back, and I take responsibility for my part in that. Would you consider giving it another try?"

Cire looked away with a guarded expression. "I don't want to mess things up. I know you're a good person and a damn good cop. That's why I called you about the laptop. I don't know, Leticia."

Leticia reached out and hugged his bicep. She was quiet for a moment. "I understand your hesitation, Cire Mohammed. I still care about you. We could be good together, and this time, no questions, cool?"

Cire met her gaze. "How 'bout we give it a try but go slow?"

The detective took a deep breath and smiled. "Slow is good. We'll figure it out together."

"Respect."

HOMECOMING

The house felt different. It felt like years since everyone was in here altogether. Things felt shady for a minute, but that was due to Alana planning a surprise birthday party. She went through extremes with my crew to help her orchestrate that. My paranoia and being involved in too many missions to count got the best of me when I thought Alana was cheating on me when she was just helping a coworker who got caught up in some serious shit with some corrupt people, including the mayor.

I rolled up my sleeves, tending to the grill pan as the sweet, smoky scent of Filipino barbecue filled the kitchen. I caramelized some onions and mixed them with minced garlic and brown sugar. Adding some other ingredients to the top of the marinade, I soaked the chicken breast in the bowl and added some banana ketchup and soy sauce. I couldn't remember the last time I prepared a meal, let alone one of Alana's favorites, but I was going to get it right.

The jasmine rice was simmering when I heard the front door open. I skipped through our common space, the living room, and stopped just in time to see Alana step inside. She hesitated, looking around the entryway as if she was waiting for me to invite her in. Sara stood next to her mom, clutching her backpack and several shopping bags.

"Daddy!" Sara threw her bags to the side and launched herself at me. I caught her and wrapped my arms around her, inhaling the scent of her hair. I couldn't believe how much I missed her as the tears flowed. She hugged my neck with force, planting a soft, gentle kiss on my cheek.

"You need to shave, daddy."

"Thank you, baby. I'll definitely make that happen now that you're home."

Alana stood, watching Sara mess with my scruffiness. She sniffed a couple of times and lifted an eyebrow.

"Am I smelling what I think I'm smelling? Like, you cooked?"

I nodded with confidence towards the kitchen. "Don't sound so surprised. I made your favorite."

She walked over to me; Sara was still glued to my side. She puckered her lips, and I bent down to kiss her.

"My kiss was better than that, Mom, dang."

"She's got a point," I smirked.

Alana walked into the kitchen, peering at the food on the table. She turned with an impressed look and smiled. "This looks.... decent. It smells good, that's for sure."

"You don't trust my cooking?"

"I do," Sara interjected. "I'll set the table."

We ate, laughed, got a little serious about the recent events, and laughed some more about the mom-daughter shopping adventures. Alana said it was a memorable experience, despite the reason they left in the first place.

The scent of Filipino BBQ still lingered in the dining area long after the dinner was over. Plates sat empty on the kitchen counter, and the soft hum of the house filled the quiet space.

Sara was pooped from the day's worth of traveling and went to bed early. She said she'd make my favorite pancakes in the morning. I was putting away the remaining food, and Alana hugged me from behind.

"It's a miracle you didn't burn the place down."

"Oooh, that hurt."

"Truth hurts," Alana said, smiling at me. She hugged me tighter, caressing the small of my back. "God, I missed you."

"I missed you, too."

"You smell like pepper and sauce," she mumbled.

"And you smell like home."

We kissed more and stumbled toward the bedroom. I picked her up, carrying her the rest of the way to the bed, laying her down as the night lamp cast a shadow of us on the wall.

We undressed. We didn't speak. We didn't need to.

UNWIND

All the pieces were back in place – for the most part. Sara was glad to be back in her room and couldn't wait to show off her new clothes to her friends. Work for JG and Alana returned to normal, and despite their respective leaves of absence, they were rewarded with promotions. JG was overwhelmed and accepted immediately, but Alana declined, citing that she wanted to spend more time with her family. That made me smile.

I needed to return to some form of normalcy, too. I walked into BUCKETS, and the smell of hot wings and other greasy food wafting from the kitchen made it all familiar.

I slid onto the stool at the bar. The one I usually sit when I'm waiting for Sal. I couldn't help but glance at the seat next to me and think about Sal showing up for our meetups. He'd tell me about some excursion or mission and skip to another story about a wild party in Dar es Salaam. No matter what was happening, BUCKETS was where Sal and I would chop it up. Old friends and I nursed the memories, good and bad. I missed him more than I realized.

The wall of TVs offered a distraction of baseball and football games, as well as other channels recapping contests from the night before. A warm voice pulled me out of my thoughts, "Hey there." It was a young woman who looked familiar to me, but I couldn't place her. She slid a menu and a coaster in front of me. Her name tag read "GINA," but something seemed different.

"What can I get you to drink?" she asked. She smelled like she'd been spritzed with a peach mist.

I squinted at the name tag and chuckled. "Gina, huh? Your sister works here, too, right?"

She smiled for a beat, blinking and shaking her head, laughing and surprised. "You're good," she said. "Nope, I'm not Gina. I'm Janice, and Gina's my twin, but she doesn't work here anymore."

"Really? What happened – if you don't mind me asking?"

Smirking, Janice leaned on the bar, exposing extra cleavage, and I inhaled more of the peach aroma. "She broke the cardinal rule. She went out with a customer."

I sat back, "Say what? That's a rule? Like, for real? No way."

Janice nodded. "Yep, it's a real rule. Makes things weird and it's unprofessional, but this guy kept coming in, promising Gina the world – tropical drinks with the little umbrellas and all. She caved and gave him her number. She said she wasn't going to pass up a free trip."

Janice slid me a beer, and I took a sip. I couldn't remember the last time I had a beer. "That must have been one helluva smooth talker."

Janice shrugged and filled two plastic cups with water, and tossed a lemon in them. Another server thanked her and walked away.

"I thought he was a little too old for her, but Gina really took to Sal. Funny guy - always making her laugh with his stories – so that's always a plus."

I froze. My glass trembled in my hand as I set it down. For a moment, I felt numb, and the noise of the bar was replaced with the loud drumming of my heart.

"You, you said his name is Sal?" I asked, my voice barely above a raspy whisper. "How long ago was this?"

Janice tilted her head, resting a finger on her chin as she thought. "Hmm, about three weeks ago, I think? Gina said they were in Baja, Mexico, for a little over ten days, and now they're out in Newport Beach – something about a cool spot with an ocean view of all the yachts. He must be loaded."

I was shocked. A rush of adrenaline surged through me like a lightning bolt. I was dizzy. Sal's alive. Sal is alive. The words repeated in my head like a chant, disbelief warring with a hundred more emotions. I pushed back from the barstool and pulled my phone from my pocket. I scrolled through some old photos and showed Janice a picture.

"Is this him?" Janice covered her mouth in astonishment, "Yes, yes, that's Sal. You know Sal, huh?"

I nodded. "Yeah, I thought I lost him, but he's just out there living his best life; having a good time with Gina."

"Hey, they must be. I know my sister. If this guy were a box of rocks, she would have dumped him like a bad habit, but I've never seen her happier."

I couldn't wrestle with my emotions, and I lost my appetite for my favorite wings. I tossed a twenty on the bar and thanked Janice.

"I owe you big time."

Janice responded with a wink. "Anytime. See ya."

I stepped outside and let the cool air give me a makeover.

Sal is alive.

~ FIN ~

[From Book #2 – Coming Soon]

ONE YEAR LATER

The backyard was alive with laughter and the sizzle of turkey burgers and apple chicken sausages on the grill. Dressed in a casual polo and jean shorts, I flipped burgers with practiced ease. The aroma of grilled meat wafted through the air, mingling with the scent of freshly cut grass. It was a perfect day for a cookout, and I was in my element. I couldn't remember the last time we gathered in the backyard with good music, friends, and food.

This party was a special send-off for Sara, who was on her way to a prestigious Swim Academy for the summer. She would leave for USC, improve her techniques, prepare for college, and beyond. Only the elite swimmers throughout the country were invited. Some would receive invites to the Olympic trials. We were so proud of our little princesses. She asked her swim teammates and other friends over, so it was a bunch of giggling, whispering, and occasional squeals at someone's cell phone. Four boys showed up, and they huddled together in their pack, looking at their phones as well.

Alana chatted with Phil, our neighbor, who was decked in his familiar Duke basketball shorts and slides. He walked over with a Corona slipped in a Duke koozie and asked if I knew what I was doing. Cire and Leticia showed up holding hands, and that broke my death stare with Phil. We greeted each other, and Cire said they were going to congratulate Sara.

"Nice party," a voice said from behind.

I turned to see a man in a suit, looking distinctly out of place among the casually dressed guests. "Thanks, but you're a little overdressed for a cookout."

The man flashed a badge: "Agent Kurt Mason."

Raising my left eyebrow, I extended my elbow. "Chuck, nice to meet you."

"Likewise. Is there somewhere we can talk?"

"I'm kind of in the middle of flipping burgers right now," I said, gesturing to the grill.

"My partner Felipe can cover the burgers. He's kind of a grill master," Agent Mason said, nodding towards a man who was indeed dressed more appropriately for the occasion.

"At least he dressed the part," I muttered. "Can we head to your office?" Mason asked.

"Sure, this way." I led Mason through the house and towards my home office. As we approached the door, Mason spoke again.

"Don't be alarmed. Someone is waiting for us in your office."

"Oh really?" I opened the door to find a woman standing inside. She, too, was dressed like I had invited her to the party. Mason was the only kid doing his own thing.

"This is Agent Stacia Morales," Mason introduced her.

"You look familiar," I said, narrowing my eyes. "I think I saw you in the bread aisle this morning. You should have picked up some buns for me."

"Agent Morales is or has been your shadow, so to speak," Mason explained.

"My shadow?"

"Chuck, do you know Roger Boatman, also known as Rahsul Shabazz X?" Mason asked.

"Rahsul, yes, yes, a good friend. My guy from many, many moons ago."

"And you've been reacquainted with him in the last few months to a year?" Morales inquired.

"I don't know if it's been that long, but you could say that."

"Do you know where he's been?" Mason pressed.

"Roger, pardon me, Rahsul has been away."

"Incarcerated," Mason clarified.

"Yeah, man, of course, but what does this have to do with me or my shadow, Stacia, right?"

"Correct, Agent Morales."

I glanced at my watch. "Look, we've got about another five to eight more minutes before my wife starts looking for me, and if you know Filipinos, they have a temper."

"You're in danger, Mr. Barnes," Morales said bluntly.

"Danger? From who, Rah?"

"No. Danger from people who want to eliminate Mr. Boatman," Mason explained.

This didn't sit well, as I shook my head. "Look, Rah and I were cool back in the day. We ran track together in high school, stayed in touch when I was in the military but lost contact."

"We're aware, Mr. Barnes," Morales said calmly.

"Whatever he got mixed up in was or is in the past. No judgment. He served his time for his wrongdoings, and I'm sure he's just trying to make do. He is just a good guy that got caught up in a bad thing, ya know?

"We understand that, Mr. Barnes, but we must ensure a few things," Mason continued.

"Look, I don't know anything about Rah's past, his situation, or anything."

"Your safety and your wife and daughter are a priority right now," Morales emphasized.

"I don't get it. I've seen Rah a handful of times since he's been in town."

"Has he been here?" Mason asked pointedly.

"Of course, I mean, you all know that if you have someone watching me."

"We're watching you to ensure you're not harmed—for no other reason," Morales assured him.

"Harmed. Do you think Rahsul is going to hurt me?"

"As I mentioned, Mr. Barnes, Mr. Boatman was involved with a dangerous syndicate," Mason said gravely.

"I still don't know what that has to do with me."

"We believe this syndicate is tracking Mr. Boatman to clean up any mess," Morales explained.

"Mess?"

"Since his release, four to six of Mr. Boatman's family and close associates have been killed," Mason revealed.

"What?"

"It's to send a message," Morales added softly.

"Fuck! Sorry to hear that."

"Mr. Boatman must have something tangible other than information the Syndicate wants," Mason speculated.

I inhaled deeply. Since Robbie's murder, El Cucuy, and the mayor's mess, Alana taught me mindful meditation. I took a deep breath. "Do you mind me asking which syndicate?"

"I thought you never asked." Morales leaned forward slightly. "The Cyphus Brothers, or I should say, the Cyphus Family."

ACKNOWLEDGMENTS

I remember the moment I finished *Shadows & Deceit*. I sat there staring at the last page, smiling, then hollered, "In the face!" — channeling Prince Akeem from *Coming to America*. "In. The. Face!" It was a mix of relief, triumph, and exhaustion rolled into one. I was ready to dive headfirst into Book II, but I forced myself to pause and celebrate what it took to get here.

To my parents, my wife, and my kids: thank you for your patience, encouragement, and faith in me — especially in the moments when I had none left for myself. As Joel Embiid reminded us, "Trust the process."

Thank you, Pablo, for those late-night and early-morning words of uplift. You kept me grounded, sis! It's in the book.

To my editor, Vanessa Flynn — thank you for your sharp eye and steady hand. Your finesse cut where it needed to and left the story sharper, leaner, and stronger.

To Michael Sosa and the Rushmore Publishing team: you stepped in at just the right time, with the proper guidance, and opened doors I couldn't have walked through alone.

A special thank you to my mentor, Gus Edwards. When I thought I'd reached the end with a short story, you told me, "Keep going." That one push became *Shadows & Deceit*.

To Spill Bill Clemmons, my first beta reader: your pivots reshaped the story in powerful ways. Much love, LB.

To Byron Rue, my second beta reader — the Lemon Pepper Wing King and reluctant chauffeur — your encouragement and loyalty carried me further than you know.

To my cousins Keith, Keysha, and Kim: I don't remember every word of every pep talk, but I remember how perfectly they landed when I needed them most.

To Ivan Jackson, Anya Burress, Eric Dodson, Dr. Floyd Hardin, Steve "Boogie" Jarvis, Reggie "Dover Dawg" Carson, SPRING90, Dr. Kenisha Thompson, and the wider circle of D9 brothers and sisters — THANK YOU. RQQ to PSI E!

To Rory "Goodfella" Christian, Rafael Ortiz, Cloyce and Shelia Dickerson: iron sharpens iron.

To those who doubted, dismissed, or stood aside — you became the spark that kept me going. Sometimes the silence of others is its own kind of fuel. You know who you are.

And finally, to YOU — the readers. Thank you for opening these pages, for walking through them with me, and for taking the time to read this story. It means more than I can ever say.

Book II will raise the stakes higher — lies will spread wider, alliances will shift, and Chuck's search for truth will push him further than before. As De La Soul said, *the stakes are high* — and they're only climbing. Get ready for what comes next.

Peace, Love, and Happiness,

Kevin M. Scott

TheKevinMScott.com